Clint accepted a
and said, "I lied."

"About what?"

"About not coming alone."

"Does the woman mean that much to you?"

"She's my friend," Clint said. "I try to take care of my friends."

"Your friend?" Comfort said. "Your friend was in bed with the sheriff last night. What do you think of that?"

"That's her choice," Clint said.

"You don't care?"

"Not a bit. Why should I?"

"I thought—"

"You thought wrong," Clint said, "and you're thinking wrong if you think I'm going to let you kill me."

Comfort straightened up and hooked his thumbs into his gun belt.

"You ain't gonna have a choice, Adams. I'm gonna kill you because I'm faster."

Also in THE GUNSMITH series

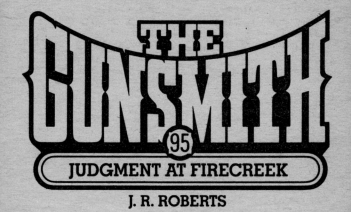

THE GUNSMITH

95

JUDGMENT AT FIRECREEK

J. R. ROBERTS

JOVE BOOKS, NEW YORK

THE GUNSMITH #95: JUDGMENT AT FIRECREEK

A Jove Book / published by arrangement with
the author

PRINTING HISTORY
Jove edition / November 1989

ISBN: 0-515-10176-1

Jove Books are published by The Berkley Publishing Group,
200 Madison Avenue, New York, New York 10016.
The name ''JOVE'' and the ''J'' logo
are trademarks belonging to Jove Publications, Inc.

PRINTED IN THE UNITED STATES OF AMERICA

10 9 8 7 6 5 4 3 2 1

PROLOGUE

The woman watched her quarry cross the street, eyes narrowed with the intensity with which she studied him. She was good with a gun, she knew that. Perhaps not as good as her partners, but more than good enough for the job at hand.

There was no paper yet on Kenny Comfort, but she knew it was coming. Her intention was to take him alive back to Winslow, Nevada, where he had killed a bank teller while robbing a bank. There was a very good chance that his cohort in that crime had been his brother, Jeff, but there was no proof of that. Kenny was the only one who had been unlucky enough to have his mask fall off. Since the Comforts had pulled several such jobs in Nevada, he was instantly recognized by the bank manager.

She had just happened to be passing through town on her way to a town called Princeton when she heard that Kenny Comfort would soon be wanted for murder and bank robbery. She had telegraphed her two partners that she was on the trail of a big one, and would continue after him if they didn't need her immediately. She wanted to make sure they got a jump on the competition. They were also on the trail of a man wanted for robbery, and since they had often split up to go after more than one bounty, her partners readily gave her the go-ahead.

She had tracked the Comforts to Firecreek, Wyoming, and this was the first sign of one of them in the two days since her arrival.

She was standing in front of her hotel and watched Comfort walk down the street and enter the White Horse Saloon. Now she pushed away from the post she'd been leaning against and walked towards the saloon. She was going to take him now, before his brother showed up. After all, he was the one with the price coming.

She checked to make sure her gun would come easily out of her holster before entering.

She knew what she looked like, and she knew the attention she would draw in a saloon, but it was early in the day yet and the place was not doing a brisk business. Several men looked up as she entered, then did a double take and watched her with admiration as she walked to the bar where Kenny Comfort was standing. As she came up alongside him he glanced her way, liked what he saw and was about to say so when she suddenly drew her gun and pushed it into his side. He looked down at the weapon and saw that it was a double-barreled shotgun that had been cut down at both the stock and the barrel so that it would fit into a specially made holster and fire one-handed. He knew if she fired he would have no insides left.

"This thing has a hair trigger, friend, so if you make the wrong move it's going to go off."

"What the—" he said. "Take it easy with that gun, lady. What the hell is the matter with you."

"You're wanted in Nevada for murder and robbery, Comfort," she said. "I'm here to take you back."

"Dead or alive?" he joked.

"One way or the other."

When he saw that she wasn't joking he began to look and feel worried.

"Lady, you got the wrong guy," he said, quickly. "Ask Paul here. He'll tell you."

Paul was obviously the bartender, a tall drink of water with a hangdog look that got even more pitiful now.

"Miss, you don't want to do this," he said, "not in this town."

"Is he or is he not Kenny Comfort?"

"He is—"

"Then I want to do it. Come on, Comfort, move."

It was Comfort himself who gave away the fact that something was amiss. Suddenly, he was looking past her and didn't seem near as worried as before.

She turned quickly and saw Jeff Comfort standing just inside the batwing doors, taking his gun from his holster. In that split second she had to assume that he was a Comfort, and that his intention was to shoot her.

She pulled the trigger and let go one barrel. The blast caught Jeff Comfort in the chest and tossed him like a rag doll. When he landed, there was no doubt but that he was dead, blown nearly in two. With him taken care of she turned her attention back to Kenny Comfort.

Kenny had a shocked look on his face and a wild look in his eye.

"That's my brother!" he shouted.

"Comfort, take it easy—" she started, but she got no further.

In his anger Comfort completely forgot about guns—his *and* hers. He reached out and grabbed her wrist, and as he jerked her towards him her gun—which did indeed have a hair trigger—went off.

The blast went right into Kenny Comfort's stomach and he bellowed out in pain. He quickly pressed both hands to the wound, but the blood simply seeped between his fingers. He looked down at himself, more shocked now than before, and then fell to the floor in a seated position, continuing to try to stem the flow of blood with his hands.

"I told you—" she started to say in frustration, but she saw that he was beyond hearing her. His eyes glazed over and he simply tilted over until he was leaning against the bar.

"Damn," she said, holstering her gun.

"Hold it right there, lady!" a voice demanded.

She turned and saw a man wearing a badge and holding a gun approaching her.

"Don't get excited, Sheriff," she said. "This man is wanted for murder and robbery in Nevada—dead or alive."

"Oh yeah?" the lawman said. "Well, you just better have a piece of paper to back that claim up, miss."

That was when she knew she was in trouble.

ONE

Firecreek, Wyoming, was the next stop on the trail that Clint Adams was presently following, but he'd found a reason to stay at least one more night in the small town of Tempe.

Her name was Louisa. She was tall and blond with clear skin, a long but graceful neck, and small, round breasts as firm as ripe peaches. Her legs were long, her thighs slender, but he knew there would be nothing skinny about them. She moved with a grace that was muscular rather than—well, *graceful*. She herself said it was from standing, waiting tables all day, and Clint didn't disbelieve it. He'd known a lot of waitresses over the years and they all had powerful legs.

He paused a moment in the street to reflect on the fact that, over the years, he had probably slept with more women who were waitresses than any other profession—if indeed being a waitress could be called a profession.

It had not been a conscious thing on his part, yet as a man who loved women—and who had loved a lot of women—he recognized the fact that he was always extremely kind, courteous and extra charming to the waitresses he met—even when they weren't particularly attractive. He found their job a particularly honest one. It required a woman who was willing to work and work hard for her money, and those women were often honest and forthright in other aspects of their lives, as well.

It might have been a terribly masculine thing to say—and some of women who were raising a ruckus over the way they were treated by men might object to it—but he had never been with a waitress who wasn't good in bed. Some were better than others, but the eagerness, the honest enjoyment of sex was always there.

He started toward the cafe again, knowing that this one, this Louisa, would be one of the better ones. They were instantly direct with each other when he had stopped there for dinner earlier that evening, and she had told him in no uncertain terms that he had better return there at one A.M. when she got off work.

She didn't have to tell him twice.

It was past one A.M. in Firecreek, and in a jail cell sat a worried gal. She still couldn't believe what the sheriff had been told in the saloon after the shooting with the Comforts. She had told her story, and then everyone—literally everyone—in the place lied and said that she had gunned down both Comfort boys without giving them a chance. They said that she had killed them in cold blood and had bragged that taking them back to Nevada dead would be much easier.

Now she lay on her cot, hands behind her head, and wondered how the hell she was going to get out of this one without help.

Without a miracle!

• • •

As soon as they entered Louisa Rosen's room, she turned and melted into Clint's arms. Her mouth was full, but not wide, and that gave her a pouty, ripe look that had attracted his attention immediately. Before he had even ordered a cup of coffee from her he had wanted to kiss that mouth.

Now he was, hungrily, as she was kissing him back. Her tongue slid into his mouth and she moaned and writhed against him. Suddenly, she pushed away from him. Her eyes were wide and she was breathing hard.

"I can't," she said.

"Why not?"

"I stink," she said. "I have to take a bath."

"Not on my account," he said. He reached for her and pulled her to him, kissing her again to make his point.

He ran his hands up her back, and then down until he was cupping her firm, hard buttocks. He slid his mouth from hers and kissed her long, smooth neck. He could smell the fried odors on her, but he also smelled her perspiration and he had discovered a long time ago that girl sweat was anything but unpleasant to him.

"God!" she said, pushing away from him then. "You don't give a girl a chance to breathe."

"Do you want to?"

"No," she said, "but I do want to get undressed."

With that she unbuttoned her uniform and hurriedly slid it up over her head. He watched as she removed her underthings, and then she stood there proudly, letting him look.

She was high-breasted, and they were hard, thrusting little breasts with rigid pink nipples. Her waist was slender, her legs as long as he had imagined, and as well muscled. He noticed that she had her hand pressed to her belly.

"Are you all right?"

"I'm fine."

"Why are you—" he said, looking at her hand.

"I'm ashamed."

"Of what?"

She looked away shyly and said, "It's ugly."

"What is?"

She hesitated a moment and then said, "My navel."

"What?" he said. "I can't imagine anything about you being ugly, Louisa. Let me see."

"No."

He moved towards her, took hold of her hand and pulled it away. He could see why she thought it was ugly. It was an outer rather than an inner. That is, instead of a shallow hole there was a nob of skin where the hole usually was. All that meant was that some doctor didn't do his job right when he cut the cord between her and her mother.

"This is nothing to be ashamed of," he said, and as if to prove the point to her he went to his knees before her and kissed it. She sighed and put her hands on his shoulders, leaning forward slightly.

He moved his mouth down slowly, seeking the place from where her musky odor was coming. He found her already wet and probed with his tongue.

"Oh, my . . ." she said. "I'm going to . . . to . . ."

"Faint?" he asked.

"Fall," she said. "You're making my legs—oh, sweet Jesus—"

He pushed her back gently until the back of her knees hit the bed and then she fell onto it. On her back she opened her long legs to him and he bent to his task avidly. He licked her, enjoying the taste of her, and then delved into her with his tongue. She wrapped her fingers in his hair as he teased her, and then found her clit with his tongue and lashed it.

"Oh, Clint, yes—it's . . . it's . . . that's it. Oh, God . . . yes!"

She began to writhe and buck beneath him, moaning and crying out, and she even turned onto her side a bit, but he stayed with her, tenaciously sucking and licking her clit until she pleaded with him to stop. He stopped, but only for a moment—long enough to stand up and discard his clothing—and then he joined her on the bed.

She immediately wrapped her hands around his stiff penis and bent to lick the head. Making joyous sounds she avidly sucked him, her head bobbing up and down, her mouth making wet noises on him until he felt the rush build in his loins. He literally pulled her mouth from him, pushed her onto her back, mounted her and thrust himself into her. She cried out and wrapped those glorious, long legs around him. He slid his hands beneath her so that he could palm her hard buttocks and as he drove into her he pulled her to him, achieving as much penetration as was humanly possible without splitting her in two.

He kissed her mouth wetly, then slid his mouth and tongue over her neck. She had the longest neck of any woman he had ever known, and yet it was perfect for her. She knew it, too, which was why she wore her hair short, so that everyone could see.

His mouth was still on her neck when she wailed and began to reach her orgasm. She started pounding on his back with her fists and drumming her heels on his buttocks, but he was oblivious to everything but

the feel of her smooth skin on his lips, and the fury
of his ejaculations as he came and came again . . .

Clint stayed the night. During parts of it they
talked, and he found out that she was twenty-five,
had been working and living there for only four
months, and had plans to leave as soon as she saved
up enough money.

"San Francisco?" he asked.

She lifted her head from his chest to look at him
and then said, "How did you know?"

He was about to answer without telling her that
most waitresses—and clerks, and saloon girls, and
whores—he had met while traveling throughout the
West were saving their money to go to San Francisco, or New York, or even Europe when she cut
him off.

"Don't tell me. I know. You've heard it all
before."

"I have, yes."

"And did any of the girls you've heard it from
before ever make it to San Francisco?"

"Some," he said, sure that at least one or two
must have.

"Then that's all the encouragement I need," she
said. "You've kept my dream alive, Clint."

"I'm glad."

She reached beneath the sheet and wrapped her
hand around his semi-erect penis.

"And that, my dear girl," he said, reaching for
her, "is all the encouragement I need."

She smiled and said, "Oh, I was hoping you
would say that, Mr. Adams."

•   •   •

In the morning she rose early with him. They made love one more time, and then she walked with him to the livery stable to pick up his rig and team and Duke, his big black gelding.

"I'm sorry you can't stay longer," she said.

He gave her a gentle smile and said, "If I stayed longer I might not want to leave at all."

"That's a hell of an excuse," she said good naturedly. She kissed him one last time and then he climbed aboard his rig.

"Don't come back this way again to see me," she told him.

"Why not?"

She smiled and said, "Because I won't be here, that's why."

San Francisco, he thought, and shook the reins to start his team.

He hoped she was right.

TWO

It was only half a day's ride to Firecreek. From all he had heard Firecreek was a growing town, and he figured a growing town should certainly have some use for a traveling gunsmith.

Clint Adams loved working with guns—that is, cleaning them, repairing them, modifying them. There was a time, years and years ago, when he even liked using a gun, but all the would-be gunmen and would-be legends had driven that out of him by hounding him until he had only one way to get away from them—killing them before they killed him.

He shook all thoughts of killing from his mind as he directed his rig down the town's main street. It was indeed a growing town, evidenced by the crowded street, the repairs being done to old buildings, and the new buildings that were being erected.

He found the livery stable at the end of the street and made arrangements to have the rig, team and Duke cared for. In Duke's case he made extra sure that he would be properly cared for by stressing the importance to the young liveryman.

"Mister," the young man said, "I may be young, but I know good horse flesh when I see it, and I know how to care for it. If you don't believe that, then you might as well take your business somewhere else.''

Clint studied the man. He couldn't have been more than twenty-two, but he had sand. He was tall and gangly, and if he ever filled out to his pride and backbone, he'd make a fine looking man.

"Is there another livery in town?" Clint asked.

"Yes, sir. It's just down the—"

"Never mind," Clint said, handing Duke's reins to the young man, "I like it here."

The man nodded and accepted the reins.

"Shall I pay you in advance?" Clint asked.

"You pay me when you're satisfied, mister."

"What's your name?"

"Will Moore."

"My name's Clint Adams, Mr. Moore," Clint said, extending his hand.

Will Moore shifted the reins to his left hand and shook hands with Clint.

"Be staying in town long?" Moore asked.

"A couple of days, maybe more. This town have a gunsmith shop?"

"We got a gun shop, but no gunsmith. Is that what you do?"

"That's what I do."

"I got an old Navy Colt my father left me, it's got something wrong with it."

"You get it and I'll take a look at it."

"Wait here."

Moore took Duke inside the livery and returned several moments later with the Navy Colt. On the surface the gun seemed well cared for, but he wouldn't know what the insides looked like until he took a more detailed look.

Moore handed Clint the gun and asked, "Should I pay you in advance?"

Clint grinned and said, "You pay me when you're satisfied."

Moore grinned and said, "Fair enough."

Clint obtained directions to the nearest hotel, stowed Moore's Colt in his saddlebag and left. Moore also told him if he wanted dinner the hotel dining room was one of the best places in town.

Clint found the hotel with no trouble and checked in. He went to his room and found it nicely furnished, though not fancy. The clerk had also told him to ask him if he needed anything. Clint was more used to having his key thrown at him and sleeping on a saggy mattress in a sparsely, and inexpensively, furnished room. He sat on the mattress and found it to his liking.

On his way through the lobby to the dining room the clerk asked if everything was all right and Clint allowed as how it was.

The treatment he got from the waiter was much the same as he had gotten from the clerk. They both gave the impression that no request was too small for a guest of the hotel. All Clint requested was a thick steak and a strong pot of coffee, an easy enough request for any dining establishment.

It proved more than easy for the hotel as the steak was tender and red, while the coffee was black and strong. In addition there were hot biscuits, boiled potatoes, and to top it off the cook had put some bacon strips on top of the steak.

He'd found places that made good coffee and he'd found some that made fine steak, but he had rarely found one place that did both.

Yes, sir, Firecreek was starting to look like a place he might not mind spending a little time.

Now, if only he had Louisa waiting on him instead of a bald waiter, things would be just about perfect.

Things were looking worse and worse from a cell in the Firecreek jail.

The lady bounty hunter who had killed the Comfort boys was looking at only her second night in jail when the sheriff came in and gave her the bad news.

"Looks like the judge won't be coming for about a week, missy."

"I thought the circuit judge was supposed to come in this week?"

"Looks like your gonna be my guest a little longer," the lawman said. "It seems Mr. Comfort requested a particular judge for your case, so we'll have to wait a little longer for him."

"What judge?"

"Judge Winston Taylor."

Judge Taylor!

"I see you know him."

"I've heard of him," she admitted.

"What have you heard?"

"That he hates bounty hunters."

"*And* women," the sheriff said. "Don't forget that he hates women."

"I see," she said, getting the picture. Well, at least Comfort was going after her within legal means, and not coming after her to lynch her. Judge Taylor may have hated women and bounty hunters, but he was still a judge, wasn't he? He was paid to be impartial during a trial and rule just on the facts, wasn't he?

Sure, he was. As if there wasn't enough money in

the world to buy a judge—one who already hated women and bounty hunters.

Yep, things were looking worse and worse.

After dinner Clint went to the nearest saloon, an establishment called Sister Kate's Saloon. The name alone was enough reason to go inside.

It was past seven P.M. and business looked good. So good, in fact, that he wondered what the place would look like at about ten o'clock, when most saloons were doing their best business.

He found some elbow room at the bar and ordered a beer, then relaxed and began to listen to some of the conversations that were going on around him. He'd always found that the best way to find out what was going on in a town that was new to him.

Usually when he opened his ears like this, he heard anywhere from two or three to as many as five or six different topics being discussed. This time, however, everyone seemed to be talking about the same thing.

It seemed that a man named Comfort was fairly big in town, and his two sons had been shot down the day before in this very saloon. That wasn't so unusual. Men were shot in saloons all the time. What made this instance so different was that they were shot down by a woman.

A woman bounty hunter.

Clint paused with his beer halfway to his mouth and thought about that. How many women bounty hunters could there be in the country? He'd personally met four. Did that mean that the odds were good that the woman in jail here in Firecreek was one of those four?

It didn't have to mean that. It could have been another lady bounty hunter, entirely.

Still, for a man who personally knew four lady bounty hunters to just calmly drink his beer when he heard that a lady bounty hunter was in jail—well, that just wasn't possible.

Not when a man's curiosity was up.

THREE

Clint found the sheriff's office with no trouble. He entered and found a deputy sitting behind the desk, with his feet up. When Clint entered the man hurriedly dropped his feet to the ground. When he saw that Clint wasn't the sheriff he relaxed somewhat but did not put his feet back up.

"Can I help you?" he asked.

He was about thirty, with sandy-colored hair that curled up around his collar. He had the beginnings of a beard and mustache, as if he had just started growing them, or had simply not shaved in the past few days.

"I'm looking for the sheriff."

"Ain't here."

"What's his name?"

"Daniels, Sheriff Dan Daniels."

"Dan Daniels?"

The deputy smiled.

"I know. He gets ribbed about it sometimes and then gets real mad. Some folks call him Dandy Dan Daniels, and that really gets him mad."

"Why do they do it, then?"

The deputy looked confused, as if he'd never been asked that question before.

"I don't rightly know," he said, finally. "Guess some folks like to get him riled up."

"Well, I'd like to see your prisoner."

"What prisoner?"

"How many you got?"

"Just one."

"Then I'd like to see her."

"You a relative?"

"No."

"A friend."

"Well, . . . maybe."

"What do you mean, maybe? Either you're a friend or you ain't."

"Well," Clint said, "you know how women are. Maybe I'm a friend and maybe I'm not. I guess it'll be up to her to decide."

It was Clint's misfortune that the deputy had not had very much experience with women, and so he didn't know how women were.

"What's her name?"

"You must know her name, Deputy," Clint said.

"*I* know her name, friend," the deputy said, "I want to see if you do."

Clint wouldn't have given the deputy credit for being that smart. He'd underestimated the man and played the situation wrong.

"Well, the truth of the matter is this—"

"You don't know the lady."

"I won't know if I know her until you tell me her name."

"Maybe you ought to wait to see the sheriff."

"Where is he?"

"Home having dinner, I guess."

"Having dinner home, or in some cafe?"

"Don't think the sheriff's wife would take too

kindly to him having dinner out when she's got it
waiting home for him."

"No, I don't guess she would. Where does he
live?"

"Yellow house down the south end of town," the
deputy said. "You can't miss it, but he'll be real put
out if you bother him during dinner."

"That's all right," Clint said, moving towards the
door, "I'll just explain that it's your fault."

"Hey—" the deputy shouted, but Clint went out
the door without looking back.

As the deputy had said, Clint couldn't miss Sheriff Dandy Dan Daniels' house. Not only was the
house yellow, but so was the wooden fence that
surrounded it.

It was late and Clint hoped that the sheriff was
finished with dinner. He really didn't look forward
to trying to deal with the man if he was as easily put
out as the deputy indicated. It might have paid to
wait until morning, but he was just too curious about
who it was they had locked up in jail.

He went up to the front door and knocked. He
heard the measured footsteps approaching the door
inside. Then the door was opened by a man wearing
a napkin around his neck. Beneath a heavy mustache
his mouth was moving, still chewing his food.

"Yeah, what?" he asked.

Sheriff Daniels was in his forties, a tall, broad-
shouldered, competent looking man with penetrating
gray eyes. Right now those eyes were glaring at
Clint, who guessed that he had interrupted the man
during his dinner—or, at least, his dessert.

"I'm sorry to bother you sheriff, but I wasn't
getting much cooperation from the deputy in your
office."

"Sounds like Zack is doing something right for a change."

Fine, Clint thought. They just weren't going to get off on the right foot.

"My name is Clint Adams, Sheriff, and I'd like to see your prisoner."

From the sheriff's reaction—narrowed eyes, a curious, appraising look in them—Clint knew that he recognized the name.

Finally the man said, "What the hell would the Gunsmith want to see a murderin' lady bounty hunter about?"

FOUR

"It sounds to me like you've already got her convicted," Clint said.

"As good as," Daniels said, wiping his mouth with his napkin. "I'm having my dinner, Adams—"

"I'm sorry to interrupt it, but it's kind of important that I see her."

"Why?"

"Well, . . . for one thing, to see if I can help her."

"Why would you want to help her?" Daniels asked. "Do you know her?"

Here we go again, Clint thought.

"Sheriff, I heard that you had a lady bounty hunter in your jail for killing two boys. Now, I know a couple of lady bounty hunters, and I'm curious about whether or not this is one of them."

Daniels pulled the napkin from around his neck and held it in his left hand. Now that the napkin was gone Clint could see the man's badge and it had a nice shine to it.

"I can't let you see her."

"Why not?"

"You ain't family, and you ain't friend."

"I won't know if I'm a friend until you tell me her name."

"You'll find out her name when we take her to court. Now, if you'll excuse me—"

"Wait a minute!" Clint said, putting his hand out to stop the door from closing. "When will she be going to court?"

"Soon as the judge gets here."

"And when will that be?"

Daniels shrugged.

"A week, maybe a little more."

"Why so long?"

Daniels sighed impatiently.

"That's when he gets here, Adams. Even a hot-shot, big rep like you can't get him here any sooner."

"Who is this judge that you're waiting for?"

"Judge Winston Taylor."

"Judge Taylor!" Clint knew the name. "He hates bounty hunters."

Daniels smiled tightly and said, "And women. Now, if you'll excuse me, Adams, I'm keeping my missus waiting."

The sheriff had a very self-satisfied look on his face when he closed the door.

Clint turned and walked away from the house. With Judge Taylor set to preside at the hearing it was even more imperative that he found out just who was in that jail cell.

And he knew a way to do it.

Clint went to his hotel and approached the desk where the very helpful clerk was standing.

"Yes, sir," the man said, "what can I do to help you this evening?"

"I'd like to see your register for the past week."

"Oh? Why is that, sir?"

"I understand a friend of mine might have passed through your town during that time. I'd like to see if I find his name."

"Oh, I see. Well, I don't see the harm in that. Here you go," the man said, reversing the register so Clint could read it.

Clint turned back the pages, reading down the list of names. He didn't have to go very far before he found a name he knew.

"Did you find your friend, sir?" the clerk said.

"Yes," Clint said, pushing the book back across the desk. "Thank you."

"You're welcome, sir."

Clint turned away from the desk and walked outside. He stopped on the boardwalk in front of the hotel and leaned against a pole. Now that he knew for sure who was in the jail cell, it was absolutely necessary for him to get in to see her.

One way or another he was going to have to get Katy Little Feather out!

FIVE

Clint had met Katy Little Feather and her two partners, Sandy Spillane and Anne Archer, within the span of one week. They had planned it so, to try and enlist his aide in hunting down a dangerous gunman named Bill Wallmann. He had become very fond of all three women, with a special feeling for Anne Archer. He had also worked with all of them since then on separate occasions.

As best as he could figure, Katy Little Feather had no chance whatsoever of a fair trial in the town of Firecreek. The sheriff was against her, the judge would most surely be against her, and the witnesses were lying. Knowing little about the men she shot, he was sure she must have had sufficient provocation. He knew she was not quick on the trigger. She was a levelheaded young woman who used her gun only when she had no alternative.

It was obvious that the sheriff was not going to let him talk to her. He had two options. He could go ahead and break her out, in which case they'd both be fugitives, or he could try and find some way to talk to her.

He stepped down from the boardwalk in front of the hotel and walked to the jail. He stopped in front of it, then continued on until he came to an alley. He walked down the alley until he was behind the row of buildings that were common with the jail and walked along the back until he felt he was behind the jail.

There was no window.

So much for that idea.

He went back to the hotel and up to his room. From his saddlebag he took his little Colt New Line. He unbuttoned his shirt and tucked it into his belt, then buttoned the shirt over it. Satisfied that it could not be seen he once again left the hotel and walked to the sheriff's office.

When he entered he saw the same deputy—the sheriff had called him "Zack,"—sitting behind the desk, a bored expression on his face.

"Zack, the sheriff wants to see you right away."

"What?"

"I said—"

"I heard you," the deputy said, squinting suspiciously at Clint. "Let's say I don't believe you."

"Well, I just spoke to him and he asked me to tell you that he wanted to talk to you."

"Says you."

"Zack," Clint said patiently, "how would I know your name if he hadn't told me when he asked me to bring you the message?"

Zack frowned at that one.

"Well, I guess you could have talked to him, but I'm not supposed to leave the jail unguarded."

"I'll be here."

"You'll be here?" Zack repeated. "Doing what?"

"Talking to the prisoner."

"He said that was okay?"

"He did."

"Well, I can't leave you here with her—"

"You're supposed to take my gun away from me while I'm here, Zack."

"Oh," the deputy said, "well, that makes sense. All right, hand it over."

Clint took his gun from his holster and gave it to Zack, who tucked it into his belt.

"Uh, I guess I'll go over to his house . . ."

"Good idea."

Still unsure, Zack started slowly for the door.

"Zack!"

"Yeah?"

Clint pointed to the open gun rack and said, "Lock it and take the key with you. What good is you taking my gun if you're going to leave the gun rack unlocked?"

Zack looked sheepish and said, "You're right." He went over and locked the gun rack and put the key in his pocket.

"Thanks," he said to Clint.

"I wouldn't want you to get into trouble with the sheriff."

"That's really nice of you," Zack said, remembering how he had treated Clint earlier.

"I don't hold a grudge, Zack."

"I'll be back soon as I talk to the sheriff."

As soon as the deputy left Clint thought to himself, let's hope you don't hold a grudge, either.

He didn't know how long he had before the sheriff returned with the deputy, so he hurried back to where the cells were. There was only one occupied and when he looked inside he saw Katy Little Feather lying on her back on the cot. She was a tall, dark-haired woman wearing buckskins and moccasins, with dark skin and big dark eyes that she had inherited from her Comanche mother.

"Katy!"

She looked up at the sound of his voice and when she saw Clint she bounded off the cot in surprise.

"Clint!"

She rushed to the cell door and they clasped hands tightly.

"How did you get—"

"Never mind how I got here or how I knew you were here. I don't have much time. Tell me what happened."

As quickly as she could, she explained the situation to him.

"Sounds like self-defense."

"It would have been, but apparently Sam Comfort has this whole town so buffaloed that no one will back my story for fear of angering him."

"Then what you need is someone to talk to the witnesses and get one of them to back you."

"Good luck."

"There's got to be one person who'll back your story, Katy. That's all it will take."

"Not in this town."

"Well," he said, thoughtfully, "the other alternative is breaking you out of here and getting you to where we can talk to another judge."

"That would make you just as much a fugitive as I am, Clint."

"Well, believe me, after what I just pulled I might end up in there with you, anyway, and then where will we be?"

"You have a point."

"You call it, Katy. *If* I can stay out of jail myself,

and *if* I can find a witness who will back your story, then you've got a chance to beat this thing, Judge Taylor or no Judge Taylor.''

"Clint, not only will the sheriff and a posse be after us, but Sam Comfort and his men.''

"They've got to catch us before they can hurt us,'' Clint said. "You still riding that Indian pony of yours?''

"Yes.''

"And I'm still riding Duke. That gives us a damned good chance of outrunning them, especially if we can get enough of a head start.''

Katy didn't say anything as she pondered his offer.

"Come on, Katy,'' he said, "jump one way or the other.''

She thought a little more then abruptly nodded her head and said, "Get me out of here.''

"... are the biggest idiot that ever walked on two feet,'' Sheriff Dan Daniels was saying as he and his deputy entered his office.

"But he told me you told him my name—'' Zack was saying, but he stopped short when Clint slammed the door shut behind them.

"What the—'' Sheriff Daniels said. He turned quickly, his hand moving for his gun, but he arrested the movement when he saw Clint Adams pointing a small gun at him.

"Just stand easy, fellas,'' Clint said.

"What do you think you're doing, Adams?'' Daniels demanded.

"I'm helping to make sure that a friend of mine gets a fair trial, Sheriff.''

Clint stepped forward and relieved both men of their guns, tossing them into a corner of the room.

He also reclaimed his gun from Zack's belt and tucked the New Line away.

"Katy?"

Katy Little Flower stepped out of the back. Clint had found both the keys to the cell and her gun in a drawer of the desk.

"Take these two nice gentlemen back to your cell, will you?"

"It would be my pleasure," she said. She removed her gun from her holster and said, "Gentlemen?"

Zack eyed her nervously, but Daniels ignored her and looked at Clint.

"This is crazy, Adams," he said. "You won't get far."

"I'll keep your opinion in mind, Sheriff."

"It's not just me and a posse that will be on your ass, Adams," Daniels said as he was led to a cell by Katy Little Feather. "You're going to have to deal with Sam Comfort and all his men. It was his sons she killed—"

"In self-defense."

"She has no witnesses of that!" Daniels shouted just before Katy slammed the cell door shut.

"I know," Clint said to himself.

Katy came out of the back, holstered her gun, walked to Clint and put her arms around him. He put his gun away and held her.

"I knew only a miracle would get me out of this," she said, looking up at him. She kissed him gently on the lips and said, "Thank you."

He smiled at her, then slapped her on the ass and said, "Don't thank me, yet. We've got a long way to go."

"To where?"

He stopped short, because he didn't know the answer.

"I guess we'll have to sit and decide that once we put a little distance between us and this town," Clint said.

"Then let's get started."

SIX

Sam Comfort was a self-made man. Everything he owned he had built up from the ground himself. His huge ranch, his holdings in town, his holdings across the country, even his seat on the New York Stock Exchange, were all meant to be passed on to his three sons.

Now he only had one son left.

He sat in his office in his home, staring from behind his desk at Sheriff Dan Daniels, a man he had brought to Firecreek ten years ago to be sheriff. He didn't own Daniels, but the sheriff knew how he had gotten his job, and he liked his job. If Comfort had a hold over the man, that was it. He *liked* his job, and the life he and his wife had here in Firecreek.

"Dan, I think I've been pretty good about this," Sam Comfort said.

"You have, Mr. Comfort."

"Don't interrupt me, Dan." Comfort's tone at the moment was gentle, but Daniels reacted as if the man had shouted at him.

"No, sir," he said, contritely.

"I've lost two sons and I didn't do what I wanted to do in the first place," Comfort continued. "I didn't ride into town and string that murdering bitch up by her tits—I didn't do that, Sheriff. But now . . .'' Comfort paused, glaring at Dan Daniels until the sheriff began to fidget. "Now," he said again, "you tell me that you let her get away."

"I didn't *let* her get—"

"Is she in your jail?"

"No, sir, but—"

"Then you let her go," Comfort said. "To me, it is as simple as that." He waved away the sheriff's unspoken words of defense. "Don't try and explain it away to me, Dan. The fact of the matter is that you . . . let . . . her . . . get . . . away!"

Comfort stood up now. He was a tall man, barrell chested, powerful, imposing in more ways than one. His right arm was hard as a rock, with bulging muscles that had served him well for years. He was the arm wrestling champion of Firecreek and its surrounding regions.

On the left side, his arm was gone, lost in the Civil War, but that made him no less imposing and, if anything, even more so.

As Comfort stood, Daniels found himself taking an inadvertent step backward. The rancher's temper had been held in check until now, but Daniels had a feeling that wouldn't last much longer.

"You had better damn well get her back, Daniels!" he bellowed. "Understand?"

"I understand, Mr. Comfort. I assure you—"

"Don't assure me of anything, damn it!" Comfort said, his face suffused with blood now. "I don't have to tell you what's at stake here, do I, Dan?"

"No, sir."

"Good. I'm not threatening you, Dan, you know that, don't you."

"Yes, sir."

"Good. Now, how many men do you have riding in your posse?"

Daniels cringed inside before answering.

"Seven?"

There was a long pause as a look of disbelief passed over the rancher's face and then Sam Comfort said, "What did you say?"

"I, uh, said . . . seven . . . sir."

"Only seven men are helping you chase down the killer of my sons?"

"Well, uh, I had to put the posse together quickly, Mr. Comfort," Daniels said. "I left my deputy in town to put together a second posse in the morning."

"But you and your men are going after them now, right?"

"Yes, sir."

"All right," Comfort said. "In five minutes you'll have another seven men."

Dan Daniels knew what kind of men Comfort was going to give him. The rancher had two kinds of men working for him: ranch hands and gunhands.

The seven men he'd get would be gunhands, and they would report only to Comfort. They'd pretend that Daniels was in charge of the posse, but when they found Adams and the Indian girl they would already be under order from Comfort about what to do.

"I . . . appreciate it, sir."

"*I* will appreciate it, Sheriff, if you would find the halfbreed bitch who killed my sons."

"I will, sir."

"Then what are you waiting for?" Comfort asked. "Get the hell out of here."

"Uh, sir, there is something else you should know."

"What?"

"The man who broke her out."

"I said I didn't want to hear excuses—"

"This is not an excuse, it's about the man who helped her escape."

"Kill him," Comfort said. "Will that be so hard? Just kill him!"

"It might not be that easy, Mr. Comfort."

"Damn it, man—"

"It's Clint Adams."

Comfort paused again—another dangerous pause—and then he said, "Adams?"

"Yes, sir."

"The Gunsmith?"

"That's right."

Comfort looked down at his desk. It was times like this that the damned missing arm began to hurt.

"In ten minutes," he said to Daniels, "you'll have thirteen more men." He looked up at Daniels and said, "Kill him!"

After Sheriff Dan Daniels left the office another man entered. There was a very strong resemblance between Sam Comfort and this man, and well there should have been, because he was Comfort's son, Ben Comfort—his first, and only surviving son.

"What did he want?" Ben asked. "Somebody to do his job for him?"

"Somebody should," Comfort said. "Somebody will. I want you to handpick twelve of our best men, take them and go with Daniels' posse."

"And?"

"And when you find that bitch I want her dead."

"You want me to bring her body back here?"

"Not her body, Benjamin," Sam Comfort said, "just her tits."

Ben Comfort smiled and said, "That will be my pleasure." Not because she had killed his brothers, but because Ben Comfort liked hurting women.

"Ben," Comfort said.

Ben turned at the door and said, "What?"

"Show a little remorse."

"For who?"

"They were your brothers, for Chrissake!"

"Pa," Ben Comfort said, turning to face his father, "they may have been your sons, but that didn't make them my brothers. Besides, they were robbing banks. You knew it and I knew it. What did you expect would eventually happen to them?"

"What they did when they left here doesn't matter," Sam Comfort said. "Nobody comes to my town and guns down my sons and gets away with it."

"You should have hanged her on the spot instead of just buying yourself a judge."

"You're probably right."

Ben nodded, appreciating the fact that this was a rare moment. His father had admitted that he had possibly made a bad decision.

"One other thing."

"What's that?"

"The man with her is Clint Adams."

Ben Comfort closed the door. Sam Comfort knew that Ben fancied himself a gunman, and that this news would come as a challenge to him—a challenge he would not be able to turn away from.

Only Sam Comfort wanted him to walk away from it.

"I'm warning you, Ben—"

"The Gunsmith?"

"Don't take any chances with that man, Ben."

"The Gunsmith," Ben Comfort said, as if he were a child and someone had just mentioned Santa Claus.

"He's a dangerous man, Ben," Comfort said. "Kill him any way you can, but don't do anything foolish."

"Don't worry, Pa," Ben said, "don't worry about a thing. I know just how to handle it."

SEVEN

When they stopped and unsaddled their horses Clint searched through his saddlebags to see what he had to offer Katy to eat. All he could come up with was some dried beef jerky.

He didn't have to tell her that they couldn't make a fire, she knew that already. She was a veteran of these kind of trail situations—but this one was different. This time instead of being the hunter, she was thrust into the new role of the hunted.

"This is delicious," she said, gnawing on the dried meat.

"Are you kidding?" he asked. "What did they feed you in that jail?"

"Nothing."

"Nothing?"

"Nothing."

"I guess I didn't get you out of there a moment too soon," he said as she finished her jerky. "Here, do you want mine?"

"Yes."

She took his piece and ate that, too.

"What I wouldn't give for a cup of coffee," she said, after she'd finished that piece, as well.

"Well, we could take a chance—"

"No," she said, "we can't."

"We could huddle together for warmth."

She looked at him and said, "It's June."

"What's that got to do with it?"

She scooted closer to him and he put his arm around her shoulder.

"How are Anne and Sandy?" he asked.

"They're fine," she said. "Doing a lot better than I am, I'd wager?"

"Are they on someone's trail?"

"Yes."

"So there's no way we can get in touch with them?"

"I'm afraid not."

"Then we're on our own."

"I'm afraid so."

"I don't think you are," he said.

"I'm not what?"

"Afraid."

She remained silent for a moment, then said, "I'm not, really. I think I'm too angry to be afraid. That might come later."

"Maybe," he said.

She put her head on his chest and said sleepily, "How did you find me?"

He explained how he had ridden into town and heard about the incident, and felt he had to check it out.

"How many lady bounty hunters do you know besides us?" she asked.

"One other."

"Who?"

"Her name is Lacy Blake."

"Mmm," Katy said, and for a moment he thought

she had fallen asleep, then she said, "She rides with Jake Benteen, doesn't she?"

"Sometimes."

Clint had met both Lacy and her sometime partner Jake Benteen some years ago, and had crossed paths only with Benteen since.* He often wondered about Lacy and what she was doing.

"I've heard of her," Katy said. "She's supposed to be very beautiful."

"That's the unusual aspect of it," Clint said, tightening his arm around her, "you're all so damned beautiful."

"You say such sweet things. You know, I couldn't sleep a wink in that damn jail."

"You can sleep now, Katy."

"For a little while, maybe."

For a second time he thought she had fallen asleep and then she spoke again.

"I'm sure Anne would want me to say hello for her," Katy said, then. She was speaking of her partner, Anne Archer.

"And Sandy?" he asked, mentioning her other partner, Sandy Spillane.

"Oh, Sandy too, but especially Anne."

"Well, when you see her—when you see them both—tell them I said hello."

"Mmm-hmm," Katy said. Again he thought she was asleep and then she said, "Anne loves you, you know?"

"Go to sleep, Katy."

But she already had.

---

*THE GUNSMITH #24 & #33.

EIGHT

Sometime during the night Clint fell asleep. He didn't remember when, but he awoke with a start with Katy's warm body pressed against him. In the distance he could see that dawn was closing in on them, and he was surprised that he had slept the entire night like that. One of them should have been on watch but there was something about the closeness of a beautiful woman like Katy—her warm body, her sweet scent—that had lulled him to sleep.

Or maybe he was just getting old.

He tried to ease her away from him without waking her, but she stirred as soon as he moved.

"Good morning," he said.

She sat up and stared at him, as if she didn't know where she was, and then said, "Oh, I'm sorry."

"For what?"

"You had to sleep sitting up all night—and we should have stood watch."

"Well, I slept pretty well, thank you," he said, "and we didn't have company, so there's no harm done."

"Well, it won't happen again, I promise you. I was just so tired, and so relieved to be out of that place—"

"You don't have to explain, Katy."

He moved away from the tree he'd been leaning against all night and caught his breath when pain leaped across his shoulders and down his back.

"That was a bad position to sleep in," she said. "You should have woke me."

"I didn't have the heart, you were sleeping so soundly," he said.

"Here, let me help you."

She got behind him on her knees and began to massage some of the stiffness and pain out of his shoulders and his back.

"How's that?"

"Much better," he said, "now all I need is a cup of coffee."

"We'll have to get it along the way, somewhere," she said, standing up. "I'll saddle the horses."

"No, no, I'll do it," Clint said, but as he tried to rise too quickly his back spasmed again. Damn, he was getting old.

"I can saddle horses, Clint," she said. "Wait until the soreness is gone from your back, and then you can do some heavy work."

He sat back down and watched as she saddled both Duke and her pony. He admired the way she soothed Duke, talking to him, petting him, as she saddled him. She really knew how to handle horses.

By the time she was finished Clint was on his feet and ready to go.

They mounted up and she said, "You know, we never did discuss where we should go from here."

"Well, we could simply go to the nearest town and turn ourselves in."

She shook her head.

"From what I heard about Sam Comfort, that

wouldn't do any good. I think we have to get out of the state, Clint. We have to go somewhere where Sam Comfort doesn't have so much power.''

"Like Texas?"

"Like Texas," she said.

Clint proposed that they then head for Labyrinth, Texas, which was almost his home. He had friends there, and they could probably get this whole thing straightened out with a judge that Sam Comfort couldn't buy.

"All right, then," she said, "let's head for Texas."

NINE

Sheriff Dan Daniels, Ben Comfort and the posse made up of townsmen and Comfort's gunmen had ridden all night and had nothing to show for it.

As they had some coffee shortly after dawn, Daniels looked around their camp. The seven townsmen had clustered together around one fire while the Comfort gunmen had made another. The men from town were eyeing the Comfort men with fear and trepidation, while the Comfort men were eyeing the townsmen with contempt.

Finally, one of the townsmen broke away and walked to where Daniels was seated.

"Sheriff?"

"Got something on your mind, Seth?" Daniels asked.

Seth Holcomb was a merchant, not a gunman or a lawman. The only reason he had agreed to be part of the posse was the same reason all the others had agreed—fear of Sam Comfort.

Now, however, they were very uncomfortable being in the company of Comfort's gunhands, and this is what Seth told Daniels.

"I can understand that, Seth," Daniels said. He

tossed the remains of his coffee onto the ground and cleaned out the cup with his hand. "What do you and the others want to do?"

"We want to go back to town, Dan," Seth Holcomb said. "You have enough men here to do what you have to do."

Sheriff Daniels could have argued with the man, but the fact of the matter was he understood. In fact, he wished he could go back to town with them.

"All right, Seth, if that's what you and the others want to do."

"No hard feelings, Dan, but—"

"I know, Seth," Daniels said. "Thanks for coming this far."

Seth Holcomb nodded, clearly uncomfortable with the decision that had been made, but he and the others were not as uncomfortable about that as they were being around Sam Comfort's killers and his vicious son. In their opinion it was Ben Comfort who should have been killed, not his brothers, or half brothers.

As Seth Holcomb went back to the other store owners, Ben Comfort came over to Dan Daniels.

"What's their problem, Sheriff?"

"They've got businesses to run, Ben," Daniels said. "They're going back to town."

"That's just as well," Ben Comfort said. "They'll just be in the way when the shooting starts."

"The shooting," Daniels said. "You've already decided that there will be shooting."

Ben Comfort looked at the sheriff. At thirty he felt that the sheriff was past his good years, and would have liked to take the job on himself, if his father would go for it. Maybe this was his chance to make that move.

"Let's not dance around with each other, Sheriff," he said. "We both know what my father wants done when we catch up to Adams and the girl, so why pretend we're out here to uphold the law?"

"Sometime I have to pretend, Ben," Dan Daniels said. Sometimes, he added to himself, it was the only way he could look in the mirror.

"Well, you keep on pretending, Sheriff," Comfort said, poking his finger into the man's chest, "but when the shooting starts, don't you get in the way."

"You'd better get your men mounted up, Ben," Daniels said. "We'll have to go back to town with the others to stock up on supplies."

"Yeah, I will," Comfort said, "I'll get my men mounted up, Sheriff, only we're not going back to Firecreek."

"Why not?"

"We can get supplies just as well in Lowell, which is the next town."

"Lowell is a small town with a small trading post."

"Don't you worry, Sheriff, we'll get what we need on the way. You can go back to Firecreek with your store clerks if you want, but we're going on."

"This is my posse, Ben," Daniels said, but even he didn't believe it. Ben Comfort just smirked and walked away from him.

When they broke camp, Seth Holcomb and the other six townsmen headed back to Firecreek. Sheriff Dan Daniels mounted his horse and surveyed what was left of his posse.

And he didn't like what he saw one bit.

TEN

Clint and Katy rode to Lowell, Wyoming with intentions of staying for as short a time as possible. It was too close to Firecreek for a posse *not* to show up looking for them. They stopped just outside of town.

"I guess we have to hope they haven't been here already," Katy said. "Or maybe they're down there now, waiting for us."

"Waiting for a man and a woman," Clint said. "Let's ride in separately, Katy. I'll go down first. If I see something I don't like, I'll be back. Give me twenty minutes, and then come on in."

"All right."

"I'll take care of the supplies, you get yourself some new clothes."

"What's wrong with my clothes?"

"Get rid of the buckskin and moccasin look and buy something a little less Indian maidenish."

"Indian maiden?" she said as he rode away.

He shrugged without looking back and rode into Lowell.

Clint rode into the small town of Lowell and left Duke in front of the trading post. The town was

53

small enough that if something were out of place, it would stand out. He'd kept a sharp eye out riding in, and he inspected the street now. Also, his instincts told him that it was safe to let Katy ride in.

He left Duke untethered, knowing he wouldn't go anywhere, and went inside the trading post.

"Kin I help ya?" the old man behind the counter asked.

The man looked so old that Clint felt he'd better answer quick.

"I need some supplies."

"Well, you jest name 'em and you'll get 'em."

They were going to have to travel light, so he bought some coffee, some dried beef jerky, some canned fruit, some bacon and some beans. He had the man split it and put it into two sacks, figuring that he and Katy would each carry one.

He was paying for the supplies when Katy walked into the place.

"Kin I help ya?" the old man asked her.

Ignoring Clint she asked, "Is there anyplace in town I'd be able to buy some clothes?"

"Yes, ma'am," the man said. "Right here."

She looked around and said, "No, I mean women's clothes."

"I'm the only place in town that sells clothes, but all I got's shirt and jeans."

"Anything that would fit me?"

The man eyed her appreciatively and said, "All I kin do, little lady, is sell you the smallest sizes I got. You'll have to make do with that."

Clint picked up the sacks and left, walking past Katy and wiggling his eyebrows.

"Take my advice, miss," he said, as if he didn't know her.

"What's that?"

"When you buy the jeans, put them on and then soak them. They'll shrink down around you."

"Thanks."

As he left Clint heard the old man say, "That feller's right, miss . . ."

Clint mounted up and directed Duke out of Lowell, leaving at the opposite end from the way he entered. He stopped just outside of town and dismounted, waiting for Katy. She rode up about fifteen minutes later with a bundle wrapped in brown paper under her arm.

"Is that your new wardrobe?" he asked.

She dismounted and said, "Jeans and a shirt. At least my own clothes fit."

"And they're very distinctive. You'd better change, Katy."

"Right here?"

"Why not?"

"You wish. I'll be right back."

She took her new clothes and went behind a bush. He waited patiently while she changed and when she reappeared she looked comical—both her clothes and her expression.

"What's the matter?" he asked.

"Look at me," she said. She spread her arms and dropped her buckskins to the ground. The shirt tail was out and hanging almost to her knees. The pants were baggy and dragging on the ground.

"You do look, uh . . ."

"Don't you dare laugh, Clint Adams. This was your idea!"

"You're right, you're right, and I'm going to do something about it. Do you have a knife?"

"In my saddlebag. What are you going to do?"

He took the knife out of her saddlebag and said, "I'm going to create for you the latest Paris fashion."

ELEVEN

When the posse, which Sheriff Daniels had started thinking of as the Comfort lynch mob, entered Lowell they rode directly to the trading post.

"Les," Ben Comfort said to one of his men, "pick up the supplies we need from the post. The sheriff and I will question the owner."

"About what?" Daniels asked.

Comfort gave Daniels a pitying look.

"If Adams and the girl passed through here they would have stopped for supplies. They did leave town in a hurry, you know." Comfort turned in his saddle and called out, "The rest of you stay out here."

"How about a drink, Ben?"

"I'll fetch a bottle," the man Comfort had called Les said.

"No, you won't," Comfort said. "No booze until this is over. You all better understand that, or you'll be looking for new jobs."

"All right, Ben," Les said, "don't get all riled up. We understand."

"Get those supplies," Comfort said.

Les, Comfort and Daniels all entered the trading

post. The old man behind the counter said, "Kin I help you gents?"

"My friend will get what we need," Ben said. "The sheriff and I need to ask you a few questions."

"Questions?" the old man asked. He cast a wary eye at Les, who was going through his shelves none to gently. "About what?"

"A man and a woman who might have passed through here today," Comfort said. "Have you seen them?"

"You ain't told me what they look like," the old man said. Les dropped something to the floor with a loud crash and ignored it as he reached still higher for what he wanted. "Hey, you," the old man shouted.

"Old man," Comfort said, reaching across the counter and taking hold of his shirt front, "pay attention over here."

"He's breaking—"

"I'll break something if you don't pay attention," Comfort said, "and it won't be something you can fix easily. Understand?"

Clearly, the man did not understand. He looked to the sheriff with puzzlement in his eyes, but there was no help coming to him from Dan Daniels.

"Now," Comfort said, releasing the man, "did you see them?"

The old man looked over at the man who was now clearing his shelves, dumping everything he didn't want onto the floor, and answered, "There was a man and a woman here earlier today, but they wasn't together."

"They wanted you to think they weren't together," Ben Comfort said. "What did they buy?"

The old man shrugged and said, "Just some

supplies—I mean, the man bought supplies, the woman bought some clothes.''

''What kind of clothes?''

''Shirt, jeans, all too big for her.''

Comfort looked at Daniels and said, ''She's trying to change her appearance.''

Daniels didn't say anything. He was wondering what Sam Comfort would do to him if he resigned as sheriff and left town.

''Could you stop him now?'' the old man said to Comfort.

Ben Comfort looked over at his man, Les, and called out, ''Do you have everything you need?''

''Well,'' Les said, dragging a sack behind him, ''there ain't no women here, so I guess this'll have to do.''

Comfort said, ''Wait outside.'' He looked at the old man and jerked a thumb at the sheriff. ''We're an official posse, old man, so we're appropriating the supplies we need.''

Comfort turned around and walked out. The old man looked at the badge on Dan Daniels' chest, and then at Daniels' face. If he was looking for some words of wisdom, or comfort, they weren't there.

Daniels looked around at the mess Ben Comfort's man had left behind and said, helplessly, ''I'm . . . sorry.''

The waiting was going to kill Sam Comfort. He knew that, so he decided not to wait. He had one of the men saddle his horse and outfit him, and he took out after Clint Adams and Katy Little Feather himself.

For his part, the trail was easy to follow.

TWELVE

Clint Adams had not intended to make love to Katy Little Feather. It was not as if they had not made love before. They had. It had simply not entered his mind that they would end up doing so. If it had been Anne Archer, there would have been no question, but with Katy that was not the case.

They rode into the town of Wet Springs, Colorado and decided to take a hotel room.

"We need the rest, and so do the horses," Clint said as they rode into town.

"What if they catch up to us while we're here?"

"That's a chance we'll have to take," Clint said. "Besides, we must have at least a day's head start on them. They couldn't have picked up our trail during the night."

"That's only about a six-hour head start."

Clint shook his head.

"The sheriff would have had to go and talk to Comfort before he left the county to come after us."

"So?"

"Comfort would insist that he take some of his men along in the posse."

"If Comfort's men are part of the posse, then it's not a posse, it's a hanging party."

"Whatever it is," Clint said, "we can afford to rest up here, and reevaluate our position."

"Reevaluate how?"

They were approaching the livery stable and Clint said, "Let's go over it later."

She nodded, and they turned their horses over to the liveryman and went to the hotel to rent a couple of rooms. They both noticed the funny looks the liveryman was giving Katy and knew that it was because of her ill-fitting clothes, but neither commented on it.

"Only got one room," the clerk said.

"Something going on in town?" Clint asked.

"We're just full up," the clerk said. "We're a growing town."

Clint thought it more likely that the hotel was too small to accommodate the size of the town now. If it grew anymore, they'd have to add rooms, or build themselves another hotel.

"All right," Clint said, "the lady will take it."

"Fine," the clerk said.

"Where will you sleep?" she asked.

"I'll find a place."

"You can share—"

He held up his hand to her and she fell silent. They signed her in and then he walked her up to her room. The desk clerk had been giving her the same kind of looks that the liveryman had, but neither of them commented on it.

"You can stay here with me, Clint," she said. "It's not as if we're strangers."

"No, I guess we're not," Clint said, "but—"

"Don't start worrying about my reputation," she

said. "I'll probably never come to this town again, and even if I was to, I don't care what they think. I don't care what anybody thinks. I do what I want."

"Stubborn."

She smiled and said, "As a mule."

"All right," he said, and he dropped his gear to the floor.

Over dinner in the crowded hotel dining room they discussed their options.

"Going to Texas will take too long," Clint said. "That decision was made in haste. I think we're going to have to find someplace closer."

"Like where?"

"Denver, maybe," he said. "We're only about a hundred miles from there now."

"We could make that in two days," she said. "What do we do when we get there?"

"Talk to the police, and to a judge—an honest judge."

"Do you know one?"

"I know some people there," he said, "and they'll know one."

She paused over her steak.

"You don't think Comfort has connections in Denver?"

"He probably has," Clint said, "but we've got to have a destination, a realistic destination. We can't just run to nowhere."

She moved her eyes around the room and saw that some people were watching them.

"I saw them, too," he said, grinning.

"Clint, I've got to get some new clothes."

"All right," he said. "After dinner you go shopping."

"Where are you going to go?"

He shrugged and said, "I'll amble over to the saloon and see what I can hear."

"What if the word has gotten this far, ahead of us," she said.

"If it has, I'll find out."

"Maybe we should stay off the street."

"You do your shopping and then go back to the room," he said. "I'll meet you there."

"All right," she said, and attacked her steak with renewed vigor.

Clint went to the saloon after he and Katy separated outside the hotel. He had a beer and listened to the conversations as well as he could. The saloon was crowded and it was kind of difficult to separate one conversation from the next, but his ears were attuned to one name—Comfort—and it never appeared —which didn't mean it wouldn't eventually, but he couldn't stay around all night to find out. Katy's suggestion that they stay off the street and out of sight was a wise one, and he decided to follow up on it.

"A bottle," he told the bartender.

The man nodded and handed him an unopened bottle. He paid for it, and tried to remember if he'd ever seen Katy Little Feather take a drink before.

Indians weren't supposed to be able to handle liquor.

Well, maybe he wouldn't give her any.

As he was leaving he suddenly heard the word, "Comfort," and turned quickly to see if he could spot who had said it. He stood just inside the batwing doors, waiting for the word to be uttered again, but finally decided it would be prudent to leave rather than stand there and attract attention.

Maybe somebody was just describing one of the saloon girls.

Sure.

THIRTEEN

So even though Clint was sharing a room with Katy Little Feather—and a bed—he still had no intentions when he went back to the room of making love to her.

Katy, knowing how Anne Archer felt about Clint, also had no plan to do anything more in bed then sleep.

When Clint entered the room he told her about hearing the name Comfort in the saloon. Katy looked concerned.

"What if someone gives us away?" she asked.

"I don't think anyone can, Katy," he said, "but maybe we should set watches. I'll take the first."

"Where?"

"In that chair," he said, indicating the straight-backed wooden chair by the window.

"Your back will get stiff."

"I'm not going to sleep in the chair," he said, putting the whiskey bottle on the windowsill.

"What's that for?"

"Just in case one of us wants a drink," he said. He considered asking her at that point if she drank whiskey, but decided against it. If she didn't, she wouldn't ask for any, and if she did, he'd know soon enough.

He noticed that Katy was standing awkwardly by the bed, watching him.

"What's wrong?" he asked.

"Nothing," she said with a quick shake of her head.

"Go to bed, then."

"Right."

She pulled the covers down, sat on the bed, removed her moccasins—she hadn't been able to find a pair of boots that fit—and proceeded to lie down between the sheets . . . fully dressed.

"Katy," he said, "you're not going to sleep in your clothes, are you?"

"Why not?" she asked. "I bought new ones, ones that will fit. In the morning I'll just leave these behind."

"You won't be comfortable . . . oh, I think I see."

"See what?"

"What I'm not supposed to see," he said. "Look, I'll turn my head and you get undressed and into bed."

"I didn't buy any bed clothes."

"I won't look," he said, turning his head away. "I promise."

He even averted his eyes from the window, so he wouldn't see her reflection in the glass. He stared at a wall and eventually heard her rise, undress and slide back between the sheets. She made a different sound this time as it was flesh that rubbed against the sheet and not cloth.

"All right," she said.

He looked at her and saw her lying in bed with the covers to her chin.

"What about you?" she asked.

"What about me?"

"When you go to sleep."

"I'll just shuck my shirt and pants," he said. "I've slept that way many times."

He stood up and crossed to the lamp on the wall by the door. He lowered the flame, then returned to the chair by the window.

"Go to sleep," he said.

She turned over, presenting him with her back. Against the sheet he could see the contours of her back and butt, and looked away. He thought back to the first time they had met, when they had made love, and then pushed those thoughts from his mind. It wasn't easy to keep looking out the window when you were in a room with a lovely woman who was naked and in bed.

But he gave it his best try.

After an hour Katy turned over in bed and looked at Clint. He heard the move and looked at her.

"What's wrong?" he asked.

"I can't sleep."

"We're safe here, Katy," he said, "for the time being, at least. We'll get an early start in the morning."

"I have the impression that this stop is for my benefit."

"That's silly," he said.

"Is it?" she asked.

"I know the line of work you're in, Katy, and I know what kind of hours it demands, many of them spent on the trail. You're not some woman who's been forced to ride sidesaddle for fifty miles and needs a soft bed to sleep in to ease the ache in her, uh, fanny.''

"I'm a woman, though.''

"So?''

"I know how you feel about women.''

"You do, huh?''

"We all do.''

"All?''

"Anne, Sandy and me. We talk about you, you know.''

"Do you? Why?''

"Because none of us has ever met another man like you. We've all . . . been made love to by you, and we've . . . made love with other men . . .''

Clint tried not to think about Anne Archer in bed with another man.

"What are you trying to say.''

"I'm trying to compliment you.''

"Embarrass me, you mean.''

"It's just that . . . we've never known a man who thought so much of us . . . of women, in general.''

"I can't apologize for that,'' he said. "Women are special.''

"All women?''

"Yes . . . some more than others, maybe, but . . . yeah . . .''

"That's what I mean.''

"What's this got to do with you not being able to fall asleep?''

She was silent for a moment, and then said, "I keep thinking about when we first met . . . when we . . . oh, hell,'' she said, turning her back to him again. Her voice was muffled as she continued. "I'm making a total fool of myself.''

"No, you're not,'' he said. He got up from the

chair and walked to the bed, but didn't touch it.
"You're just being truthful. I'm thinking about that
time, also."

She turned over and looked at him. Although the
lamp was low he could see her eyes, large and
brown, studying him.

"You are?"

"Yes."

They stared at each other for an awkward moment, and then Clint began to unbutton his shirt.

"Since neither one of us is sleeping . . ."

FOURTEEN

As he removed his boots and pants Katy pushed
the sheet down to her waist. Her breasts were small—
smaller than Anne's, and much smaller than Sandy
Spillane's—but they were firm and dark, with very
brown nipples.

He slid into bed next to her and she shifted her
legs so that they were on top of his. Her flesh was
smooth and hot. She reached down and took hold of
his thickening penis, stroking it.

"I hope Anne forgives me for this," she said.

"Are you going to tell her?"

"No."

"Neither am I."

Actually, there was nothing to tell her. He and
Anne were not engaged, and in fact were only
friends—albeit very good friends—but he also considered her two partners, Sandy and Katy, his friends.

He leaned over and kissed Katy, inhaling her
scent. She must have taken a bath before returning to
the room, for she smelled clean and fresh. It made
him think that he should have taken a bath as well—
and would have, if he had thought this would happen.

Her mouth was tentative at first—maybe she was

still thinking about Anne—but then it became avid,
demanding. Her tongue thrust its way into his mouth,
intertwining with his own, and her breathing came
rapidly through her nose. He slid his hand up over
her rib cage and cupped her right breast, thumbing
the nipple. She moaned and squeezed his penis tightly,
and then he rolled her over onto her back, forcing
her to release him. He began to kiss her breasts,
sucking her nipples as she moaned and ran her hands
through his hair. He slid his hand down over her
belly until he found the slick folds of her vagina, and
ran his fingers over them. She began to move her
legs and wiggle her butt, unable to keep still as he
stroked her. He kissed her again, nibbling at her
lower lip, squeezing her nipple and stroking her
pussy. She writhed on the bed and moaned into his
mouth, almost crying with the need that was welling
up inside of her.

"Please . . ." she said, pulling her mouth away
from his, "please . . . now . . ."

He rolled over on top of her and entered her in
one swift move. She was so wet and hot it was like
thrusting himself into a cauldron of boiling water.

"Oooh, yes . . ." she groaned, and lifted her hips
to meet his thrusts.

He slid his hands beneath her to cup her firm
buttocks, and the room was filled with the sound of
flesh slapping flesh, faster and faster until he groaned
mightily and she cried out as they both climaxed
together . . .

Ben Comfort poured himself a cup of coffee and
looked across the fire at Sheriff Dan Daniels.

"Daniels," he said, "why don't you just go on

back. You're not doing anybody any good here. You don't have jurisdiction anymore."

Daniels stared at Comfort for a few seconds, then tapped the badge on his chest.

"See this?"

"Yeah, I see it."

"It's a badge."

Comfort looked away unconcernedly and said, "I know what it is."

"Well, as long as I'm with you, and I'm wearing this badge, you and your killers are a posse. Without me, you and your killers are just . . . killers."

Comfort brought his eyes slowly to bear on Daniels and he stared until the sheriff started to fidget.

"Killers, huh?"

"You got another name?" Daniels asked, standing his ground.

Comfort thought a moment, then sipped his coffee before answering.

"No," he said, finally. "No, I don't. I kind of like yours. Killers," he said, thoughtfully, "yeah, I kind of like that one."

In the morning Clint and Katy had an early breakfast. The hotel dining room hadn't opened yet, but they found a cafe that had.

As they saddled their horses in the livery Clint said, "We could use some more supplies, but I don't want to wait for the general store to open."

"We'll pick them up in another town."

He nodded, and they both mounted up.

"Clint," she said, before they started out.

"Yep?"

"About the other night . . ."

"What about it?"

"When I was in that jail I was really scared," she said, not looking at him. "I thought maybe I'd never get out. I thought maybe I was . . . you know, gonna end up . . . dead."

She paused there and he waited while she looked inside of herself for the words she wanted.

"Last night it felt wonderful to be alive," she said, finally. She looked at him and added, "I just wanted to thank you for that."

"Don't mention it."

FIFTEEN

As they broke camp Ben Comfort said to Daniels, "We're changing direction."

"Why?" Daniels asked. "We're on their trail now."

"That's just it," Comfort said. "We're on their trail and we're behind them."

"So?"

"I want to get ahead of them."

"How did you intend to do that?"

"By anticipating their next move," Comfort said. "Where are they gonna head, Sheriff?"

"Somewhere they can tell their story," Daniels said. "Someplace that isn't totally run by your father?"

"That's right," Comfort said, "and the nearest place to here that fits that description is Denver. A big city, where my father has some influence—but only some."

"So we head for Denver."

"We'll cut cross country and get there ahead of him," Comfort said.

"Adams may have some friends there, Comfort," Daniels said. "A man like that is not without influence, himself, you know?"

"What do you suggest?" Comfort asked.

"Your idea is sound," Daniels said, "but instead of getting there ahead of them, let's get between them and Denver."

"And never let them get there at all," Comfort said. "I like that, Sheriff."

"Yeah, I thought you might."

"Maybe you're worth more than just that tin star, after all," Comfort said. "I'm not convinced yet, mind you, but I'll keep an open mind from here on in."

"You do that," Daniels said.

It had been a long time since Sam Comfort had done extended time in the saddle. Comfort himself was starting to realize that. He rose that morning stiff and sore and burned his hand pouring himself a cup of coffee.

There was a time, however, when Sam Comfort could read the signs of a trail as well as anyone, and spend as much time in the saddle as was necessary. He was rusty, but he was fairly certain he was on the right trail, and he hoped to catch up to his son, the sheriff and the posse before nightfall.

If his bones didn't give out first. But when he thought about his two dead sons, he was able to ignore the aches and pains of his body.

It was the aches and pains in his heart that took over then.

SIXTEEN

Clint and Katy stopped at the next town along the way, Trinity, to buy supplies. When they came out of the general store Clint saw the telegraph office across the street.

"Do you have any idea where Anne and Sandy might be now?"

"We agreed to meet in a town called Little Chapel, in New Mexico."

"Why there?"

"We thought we'd need a rest after I brought in the Comforts and Anne and Sandy tracked down the Kincannon gang."

"The Kincannon gang?" Clint asked. "All of them?"

"There were eight," Katy said, "but Anne and Sandy were tracking Dan Kincannon and two others. All they want is Kincannon, though. The price is on him."

"Is there a telegraph office in Little Chapel?"

"No," she said. "We've been there before. It's just a small, sleepy town where we rest sometimes."

He stared at the telegraph office again.

"Let's go across the street," he said.

"Why? We don't know where they are."

"I want to send a telegram to Rick Hartman, my friend in Labyrinth, Texas."

"Why?"

"He's got more contacts then anyone I know," Clint said. "If he knows the story then the Comforts might not get away with killing us."

"If they do kill us," she said, "what does it matter whether they get away with it or not?"

"I don't know," he said. "It matters to me. Maybe I'll rest easier."

"What about sending a telegram to someone in Denver, telling them that we're coming?"

"I don't know right now who I would send it to," Clint said. "When we get there I'll decide who can help us more. For now, I'll just notify Rick."

"All right."

They crossed and Katy stood outside while Clint went in, composed his message to Rick and then sent it.

"Will you be waiting for a reply, sir?" the clerk asked.

"No," Clint said. He wanted to get back on the trail as soon as possible. The one long stop in Wet Springs was enough. "No, no reply."

Clint paid for the message and then went outside with Katy.

"All done?" she asked.

"Done."

"We'd better get moving again."

They crossed to where they had left their horses in front of the general store and mounted up.

They were two hours out of Trinity when Clint suddenly reined Duke in.

"What's wrong?" Katy asked.

"Something just occurred to me."

"What?"

"I put myself in the place of the Comforts, and the sheriff," he said. "Try it for a moment. Where would you figure we were heading?"

She thought a moment and said, "Probably Denver. Someplace big enough that we could get lost, also someplace big enough that Comfort wouldn't control it totally."

"Right," Clint said, "Denver. So what would you do if you were with that posse?"

"Try to get there ahead of us," she said without hesitation.

"Or simply try to get ahead of us," he said, thoughtfully. "Or maybe between us and Denver."

"So what do we do?" she asked. "Change direction?"

"No," he said, "Denver is still our best bet, and maybe we're wrong. What we'll do is proceed a bit more cautiously. We'll assume that they're not only behind us, but ahead of us as well."

Katy looked away for a moment, then back at him. He saw something new in her eyes.

"This is what it feels like, isn't it?" she asked.

"What?"

"To be hunted," she said. "I mean, I've been the hunter for so long, suddenly I know what it's like to be the hunted. I also know what it's like to be behind bars, thinking that there is no chance that you will get out."

"Katy—"

"If we get out of this, Clint," she said, "I think I'll find a new line of work."

"You can think that over and make your final decision after we *do* get out of this," he said.

"No—"

"Katy, don't make any decisions now," he said. "Don't even think about it now. We've got enough to do right now without losing our concentration."

"All right, Clint," she said. "Let's get ourselves out of this mess first."

From then on they would proceed cautiously, looking not only behind them but ahead of them as well.

Sam Comfort was confused.

Unless he was reading the sign wrong, Clint Adams and Katy Little Feather were still proceeding in the same direction, but the posse had changed direction. Whose decision was that, he wondered, and for what reason?

Comfort camped and made a pot of coffee, trying to decide which way he should proceed. Should he continue to track Adams and the woman, or continue to follow the posse's trail, even though they'd changed direction.

There had to be a good reason for the change. It couldn't be that they had lost the trail. For Chrissake, it was so plain that even he could read it.

He decided to stay on the trail of the woman who had killed his sons. Whatever the posse was planning —whether it was being led by Daniels or by his son, Ben—he could only guess, but he knew one thing. If he continued in a straight line, he'd find Adams and the woman, and that was his ultimate goal.

SEVENTEEN

"You know where we are?" Katy asked.

"I've been here before," Clint said.

He looked around, seeking and finding familiar landmarks.

"We're about ten miles out of Denver."

"I guess we'd better take it real careful from here on in," Katy said. "They're likely to be just ahead of us, or in Denver waiting for us."

"They'll be waiting for us," he said, "if we continue in a straight line."

"Meaning . . . what?"

"Meaning we could just circle around them and go on into Denver."

"Won't they have someone waiting in Denver for us?"

"Denver's a big place," he said. He looked at her and said, "You've never been to Denver, have you?"

"I've never been to Denver," she said, "or anyplace as big as Denver."

"Well, I think you'll find it interesting, Katy," Clint said. "Come on, it'll take us a little longer, but we'll still get there."

Instead of continuing straight on into Denver they

began to make a circle around it, with the intent of coming in from a different direction. The posse couldn't possibly be so big that they would be able to cover every entry into the city.

Once they were safe in a Denver hotel, Clint would have to decide who they would go and see.

Ben Comfort, Sheriff Dan Daniels and four other men were camped about five miles outside of Denver. The other fourteen men had been dispatched to Denver, with instructions to cover as many hotels as they could, just in case Adams and the woman got past them.

"Also the police department," Dan Daniels had said. "Make sure there's a man covering that."

Comfort's men looked to him and he nodded, letting them know that they should obey the sheriff—in this instance, anyway.

They had been camped there for over ten hours, and suddenly Daniels stood up.

"They're not coming."

"What?" Comfort asked.

"They must have gone around us," the sheriff said, "or else they'd have been here by now."

Comfort stood up and looked back towards Denver, as if he could see it from here.

"That means they may already be in Denver," Comfort said, "spilling their guts to some judge or policeman."

"See this star?" Daniels said.

Comfort had heard this song before and he stared at Daniels.

"This star means that whatever they tell a judge, or a policeman, or the man on the street, they're gonna believe me."

"You think so, huh?" Comfort said.

"I know so."

"Why?" Comfort asked. "Because you're the law, and the law doesn't lie?"

"No."

"Because you got an honest face, maybe?"

Daniels smiled and said, "That's it—and because Adams has a reputation as a gunman. Who would you believe, Ben, a lawman or a gunman?"

"You mean killer, don't you?" Comfort asked. "By gunman you mean killer."

Daniels nodded and said, "I mean killer."

"Well," Comfort said, "you might have a point there . . . Sheriff. Why don't we go into Denver and test your theory, huh?"

"Why don't we."

When Clint and Katy entered Denver they stopped at the first livery they came to.

"You know where we are?" Katy asked.

"I have an idea."

They left the horses at the livery, and Clint slipped the liveryman a few extra dollars to make sure Duke and Katy's pony were well cared for. He didn't know when they'd be getting back to them.

They left the livery carrying their gear and started walking down the street. Clint's eyes were carefully combing both sides.

"If they were smart," he said, "they would have covered all the liveries."

"See anyone?"

"No," he said. "The next smartest thing to do would be to cover the hotels."

"All of them?" she asked. "There must be dozens."

"All sizes and shapes," Clint said, "but they'll only be able to cover so many."

"How will we know which ones?"

"We won't know," he said, "we'll just have to choose carefully."

"Can we get something to eat," she asked, "or do you think they'll have all the restaurants covered as well?"

"No," he said, "we can get something to eat. There's a place, right across the street."

They crossed over and entered a small restaurant. They stowed their gear under the table and gave the waiter their order. They both ordered eggs and potatoes, and coffee.

Over the meal—it was a breakfast meal but they were eating it at more of a lunch time—Katy made a suggestion to Clint.

"You could keep going, you know?"

"Why would I want to do that?"

"I'm the one they want," she said. "I'll hand myself over to the nearest law and you can get out of this."

"What kind of a friend would I be if I did that, Katy?" he asked.

"A live one," she said. "You did your part, Clint—more than your part. You got me out of jail and away from Firecreek."

"I'm not clear of this, Katy," he reminded her. "I broke you out of jail. They want me just as much as they want you."

"They want you, but not as much," she said. "If they find me, they'll forget about you."

"Not Sam Comfort," Clint said. "He wouldn't forget that I tried to help the woman who killed his sons."

"Jesus," she said, putting her fork down for a moment, "I wonder if I could have avoided—"

"You killed them because you had to, Katy."

"How do you know that?" she asked. "How do you know there wasn't some other way I could have gone."

"Because I know you," he said. "I know you did what you had to do. Don't start second guessing yourself. All that'll do is get you killed next time."

"Next time . . ." she said, shaking her head and picking up her fork.

When they were almost done eating Clint ordered a second pot of coffee. The waiter brought it, but didn't leave.

"Something I can do for you?" Clint asked, looking up at him. He was a short man in his forties, with a hairline mustache and a protruding belly.

"You wouldn't be looking for a place to stay, would you?" he asked.

Clint sat back and said, "We might. Why? You know a good hotel?"

The man smiled now and said, "No hotel. Something cheaper."

"Like what?"

"A rooming house."

"You wouldn't happen to own this rooming house, would you?"

"I don't own it," the man said, "but my sister does."

"Where is it?"

"A couple of blocks from here. The rates are real reasonable."

Clint looked at Katy, who shrugged, indicating that it was his decision.

"When you bring me the check," Clint said, "bring me the address."

"Yes, sir," the man said happily, and moved away from the table.

"That solves our hotel problem," he said to Katy, who nodded and poured herself another cup of coffee.

"It would be nice," she said, "if all our problems were solved so easily."

EIGHTEEN

After paying the check Clint and Katy followed the waiter's directions to his sister's boarding house, which was literally just two blocks down the street. It was a wood frame building that could use a paint job, as could the wooden porch.

"It's run down," Katy said.

"That's just fine," Clint said. "It's not a hotel, and there's nobody watching it."

They went up the steps and Clint knocked on the door. It was opened by a woman who looked to be forty or so. She was handsome, with a full body that was threatening to burst from the plain print dress she was wearing. She looked at Clint, glanced at Katy, and then gave Clint a much longer look.

"Can I help you?"

"Your brother says you have a room for rent," Clint said.

She looked at Katy again, then said to Clint, "Just one room?"

Clint smiled and said, "Yes, ma'am, just one room."

She nodded and said, "This way."

She turned and moved inside and Clint and Katy followed her. She led the way upstairs and Clint watched her solid hips and rump as he walked behind her.

They followed her down the hallway of the second floor until she stopped in front of a doorway.

"This room has a double bed. I don't have any rooms with two beds."

"One bed's plenty," Clint said.

She studied the two of them for a moment and then asked, "You ain't married, are you?"

"Does it matter?" Katy asked.

The woman looked at her and said, "No, honey, it don't matter. My name's Liz, and the room's a dollar a day. I ain't gonna charge you for the two of you using it."

"Why not?" Katy asked.

Liz gave Katy a deadpan look and said, "Hell, I figure maybe you're on your honeymoon, honey." She turned to Clint and said, "One dollar."

Clint took out two and said, "Here's two days, in advance."

"Fine."

"Uh," Clint said as she started back down the hall, "do meals come with the room?"

She turned and said, "My brother deals in food, I deal in rooms." She paused, then gave Clint a meaningful look and added, "And other comforts."

"We won't be needing any other comforts," Katy said.

Liz gave her a long look, then turned and walked down the hall.

"Let's go inside," Clint said.

They entered the room and dropped their gear on the floor.

"You think that bed will hold the two of us?" Clint asked.

Katy looked at him and said, "Well, there's no time like the present to find out . . . is there?"

NINETEEN

Ben Comfort, Dan Daniels and two other men were seated in the dining room of the Denver House Hotel. The rest of the "posse" was out watching hotels, waiting for the arrival of Clint Adams and Katy Little Feather.

These four men formed the "braintrust" of the posse. Actually, Comfort and Daniels would make all the decisions, and the other two men—Hal Samuels and Del Williams—would carry the word to the other men.

"They could have found somewhere else to stay," Ben Comfort said.

"That's true," Daniels said. "A boarding house, maybe, or even a stable, somewhere."

"Or a hotel we haven't found," Comfort said.

"What can we do then, boss?" Williams asked Comfort.

Comfort looked at Daniels and said, "I'll let the sheriff tell you, Del."

Williams and Samuels looked at Daniels, waiting.

"We'll have to watch the police station," Daniels said, "and any substations they may have."

"What if they don't go to the police?" Samuels asked.

"Where else would they go?" Williams asked.

"To a judge," Ben Comfort said.

"If they do that we're sunk," Daniels said.

"No we're not," Comfort said. "Whatever they tell a judge, he would still have to contact the law back in Firecreek and hear our side of it."

"Oh, Christ . . ." Daniels said.

"What?"

"I left Zack in charge."

"That doesn't matter," Comfort said. "If the telegraph office gets a telegram from someone here in Denver, it will be shown to my father first."

"Which reminds me," Daniels said. "I'll send your father a telegraph message tomorrow, letting him know where we are."

"Fine," Comfort said.

"What about us?" Williams asked. "And the others?"

"You'll just have to tell the others to keep watching the hotels."

"All night?" Samuels asked.

"All night," Comfort said. "You two can bring them something to eat."

"Is that what we are?" Williams asked. "Messenger boys? Waiters?"

"You're whatever I tell you you are," Ben Comfort said, "aren't you?"

He stared at both men until they began to fidget in their seats.

"Now get going," Comfort said.

Both men stood and left the dining room.

When Comfort looked back at Daniels he found the sheriff staring at him, but not really seeing him.

"What's wrong with you?"

"Get them back!"

"What?"

"Get those two back!"

"What for?" Comfort demanded.

"Telegraph offices," Daniels said. "Come on, get them back and I'll explain."

Comfort looked annoyed for a moment, then got up and went after his two men.

Sam Comfort was camped, still a full day out of Denver. It had become plain to him now where Adams and the woman were headed, but it wasn't going to do them any good. They wouldn't get away from him.

It had also become plain to him why the posse had changed direction. They were trying to get to Denver ahead of Adams and the woman. It was a good move, and he was proud of Ben for having thought of it.

He was leaning forward to grab the coffee pot when he heard a noise behind him. He started to turn, but before he could do so something struck him behind the right ear, and everything went dark.

The second time Williams and Samuels were dispatched no one went after them to bring them back.

"Do you think it's wise to pull them off the hotels?" Ben Comfort asked.

"If we don't spot them tonight then it's obvious that they found a place to stay. There's nothing to be gained by watching hotels. There is something to be gained by watching telegraph offices. Instead of coming here to talk to someone they might have come here to get lost in the crowded city, and to telegraph for help."

Comfort poured himself a cup of coffee before speaking again.

"I'm allowing this, Daniels, because I agree with you. It's a good suggestion."

"Thanks," Daniels said, wryly. He knew that Comfort was saving face, here, and there was nothing he could do about it.

"You understand that?"

"Sure, Comfort," Daniels said, "I understand."

"Good," Comfort said. "We'll get along, Daniels, as long as we both remember our place."

"Sure," Daniels said. "You're a Comfort and I'm just hired help."

Comfort smiled and said, "Very good, Sheriff, *very* good."

Daniels stood up.

"Where are you going?" Comfort asked.

"To bed. I want to get an early start in the morning. You'd be wise to do the same."

"I'll go to bed, all right, as soon as I find something warm and furry to snuggle up against. Good night, Sheriff."

"Yeah," Daniels said, "good night."

Daniels went to his room, removed his gun belt and boots and sat on the bed. He hung the gun belt on the bedpost, where he could get to it easily.

He thought about what he had learned about Ben Comfort along the way, from Firecreek to Denver. The man was brutal, he had always known that, but he had never spent this much time with him before. He was learning that as long as Ben Comfort thought he was getting *his* way, that Daniels could effectively get his.

That put him back in charge of his posse—sort of.

TWENTY

Feeling the safest they had in some time Clint Adams and Katy Little Feather were able to give each other their undivided attention.

Katy was lying on her back with her legs spread wide and her arms at her sides. In each hand she had wound the bedsheet tightly, and was writhing beneath the ministrations of Clint Adams' tongue.

Clint had his face buried between Katy's legs. His tongue was avidly tasting her, his chin rubbing itself against the course, wiry black hair that surrounded her pussy.

He had his hands beneath her, cupping her buttocks and holding her up off the bed so he could drive his tongue even deeper. When she came she moaned aloud and rolled to her right, as if she were trying to get away from him. What she was doing was trying not to scream. She pulled herself away from his mouth, but he went with her and reestablished contact, continuing to manipulate her clit with his tongue until she put her hands on his head, saying, "Enough, enough . . . please . . ."

He broke the contact then and moved up to lie next to her. He began to suck her left breast while

95

squeezing the right one in his hand. Katy moaned and moved her legs, still trembling from the intensity of her orgasm.

Clint kissed her on the mouth and then propped himself on an elbow, looking down at her.

"Why did you tell me to stop?" he asked, teasing her. "Didn't you like it?"

"It was incredible," she said, "but at one point it got so sensitive. If you hadn't stopped I would have screamed the house down."

"Well," he said, rubbing her right nipple with his finger, "our landlady wouldn't have stood for that, would she?"

"No," she said, "maybe if she was doing the screaming, but not me."

"What do you mean?"

Katy smiled and put her hand over his, stopping the manipulation of her nipple.

"Don't tell me you didn't notice the way she was looking at you, Clint."

"Was she looking at me?"

"You know she was," Katy said. She slid her hand down over his belly to cup his swollen penis. "Women find you attractive, or didn't you know that?"

"Uh, I've had a clue, from time to time . . ."

"Well," she said, squeezing him, "let me give you another clue . . ."

She slid down until she was between his legs, holding his penis with both hands. The head of his penis was showing and she licked it slowly until it glistened with her saliva. She removed her top hand, exposing more of him, and leaned over and took him into her mouth.

He reached down and held her head in his hands

as she began to bob up and down. She released him
with her other hand and cupped his balls as she took
more of him into her mouth.

She continued to suck him until she felt that he
was ready to explode, and then she pulled her mouth
away, abandoning him. The air felt very cold on his
very wet penis.

She moved up so that she was sitting on him. His
penis wasn't inside of her, it was trapped between
them. In fact, she was sitting on it and she could feel
it pulsing against her wet vagina. She lifted her hips
then, reached for him and guided him into her, and
sat down on him again, this time with his full length
inside of her.

She began to move on him slowly at first, and
then faster and faster until she was literally bouncing
up and down on him. Her small breasts were so firm
that they merely rippled each time she came down
on him, but didn't bounce.

She had both hands pressed against his belly as
she continued to ride him, and her head was thrown
back so that he couldn't see her eyes, only her
mouth and chin and neck, all of which he wanted to
kiss.

When he felt her trembling with the need to come
he reached for her and pulled her down to him. He
kissed her neck, her chin, and then her mouth, and
as he thrust his tongue into her mouth he felt her let
herself go, and he went with her . . .

"What are we going to do in the morning?" Katy
asked later.

"Well, I've given that a little thought."

"When did you have time to do that?" she asked,
slapping him on the arm.

"While you were doing all the work a little while ago."

He stopped as the slap became a punch.

"All right, I'm listening," she said.

"Well, I figured I'd go to the nearest telegraph office and contact Rick again."

"What for?"

"Well, he could check and see how things were in Firecreek for us," Clint said. "He might even be able to get someone to go there and try to smooth this thing out."

"You think that can be done?" she asked. "You think we can just smooth this out with Sam Comfort?"

"Maybe not," Clint said, "but we've got to try everything we can."

"So what else, after the telegraph office?"

"Well, the smart thing for us to do would be to walk into the police station and give ourselves up."

"Why does it sound like we're not going to do that?" Katy asked.

"Because we're not."

"Why not?"

"You could do it," Clint said, "but I've got a reputation that is not always looked upon kindly by the law, especially not city law."

"What do you mean?"

"Well, a sheriff in a small town, or even in a big town, he might recognize my name, and if he does then he knows my reputation. Sometimes they're impressed, sometimes they're intimidated, and every once in a while one of them thinks he's got to show me he's not impressed."

"And what about city police?"

"Well, these fellas are different. A lot of them are from the East, where if they've heard of me it's through some cheap dime novel that was written about me.''

"So?"

"So, they don't believe what they read in dime novels. They're not going to be impressed or intimidated by my reputation."

"How are they going to react?"

"Well, they'll figure with the rep that I have that I'm probably on the run, and they're not likely to believe anything I say, especially if I'm speaking against some sort of law."

"Like the sheriff of Firecreek?"

"Right."

"And they'll believe me?" she asked. "I'm the one who killed the Comfort boys."

"You're a woman," Clint said. "They'll listen to you, and they'll check your story with Nevada."

"And where will that leave you?"

"Well, once they check your story and find out you're telling the truth maybe they'll take your word about me," Clint said. "Maybe then I'll get to tell my story."

"And you think they'll listen?"

"Maybe," he said. "Maybe they'll listen *before* throwing me into a cell."

"I don't like this idea."

"I was kidding about the—"

"There's got to be someone we can see who will listen to us—both of us."

"Well . . ." Clint said.

"Is there?"

"I know some people here."

"Who?"

"They're Pinkerton detectives."

"Pinkertons!" she said. "The police would listen to them, wouldn't they?"

"Maybe."

"Do you know Pinkerton himself?"

"Ah, yeah, I know him," Clint said, "but we're not the best of friends."

"Where did you meet Allan Pinkerton?"

"Oh, we've crossed paths once or twice. He's offered me a job with the Pinks a couple of times, but I turned him down."

"Why?"

"I don't want to work for him."

"Why not?"

"I don't like him."

"And does he like you?"

"No."

"Then why did he offer you a job?"

"I guess he respects me."

"And you him?"

Clint hesitated, then said, "To a certain degree. I respect what he's accomplished, but not necessarily the way he's accomplished it."

"Would he help us?"

Clint hesitated again, then said, "He might. We can ask. All he can do is say no."

Katy rolled over so that her head was resting on his chest.

"We'd better get some sleep," she said.

He slid his hand down her back to the rise of her smooth, firm buttocks, and ran his finger along the crease between them.

"If you really want to."

"We should get up early."

"We should."

He cupped one buttock and squeezed it.

"Mmm," she said, moving her hand between his legs. "Well," she added, thumbing the spongy head of his penis, "maybe we don't have to get up *that* early."

TWENTY-ONE

Ben Comfort rolled over in bed and bumped into something warm. He moved his hand down a smooth hip, over a soft belly and found something furry. He moved his fingers and the something furry became something wet and furry.

"Hmmm," she moaned, closing her legs over his hand. "You like it in the morning, huh?"

"I like it anytime," he said.

He pushed her legs open and moved over her, instantly hard.

"Easy, friend . . ." she said, but she gasped when he entered her brutally.

"Just lie still and enjoy it, sweetheart," he said. He slid his hands beneath her, cupped her buttocks and squeezed her—hard!

"Ow, Jesus," she cried out, "you're gonna leave bruises—ahh!"

He cut her off by thrusting into her as hard as he could, and suddenly her legs were wrapped around him and she forgot about the bruises he was going to leave on her ass . . .

Comfort was getting dressed, and when he turned and saw the woman still in bed he got annoyed. She was a big woman, standing about five ten, with huge breasts and buttocks—not fat, but big and solid. She had long dark hair and a face that was beginning to show her years, of which she had to be carrying at least forty. At her age, Comfort couldn't understand how that well packed body had not just fallen around her.

"I thought I told you to get dressed," he said.

"Honey, you just about wore me out last night, and this morning," she said. "I need to get some sleep."

"Well, get it somewhere else," Comfort said. "I'm not leaving you here to rob me while I'm gone."

"Rob you?" she said, sounding hurt. "Honey, I wouldn't—"

Comfort didn't let her finish. He took two quick steps, grabbed her arm in a painful hold and hauled her to her feet. She stood there, pulled away from him, her breasts quivering.

"That hurt!" she said.

"Try this!" he said, and backhanded her across the face. She was big and solid, though, and the blow didn't knock her off her feet. Her hand flew to her face and she glared at him.

"My man ain't gonna like it if I leave here with bruises on my face," she said. "My butt, that's fine, that's part of my work, but not my face."

"You tell your man if he don't like it he can come and find me here," Comfort said. "I'll do more than bruise his face."

She continued to glare at Comfort, then lost some of her bravado and averted her eyes.

"All right, all right," she said. "I'll get dressed and leave."

He waited while she dressed and when she was ready—wearing a simple, cheap dress that showed off her breasts—she turned to him and said, "You gotta pay me."

"I'll pay you," he said. He took some money from his pocket, walked up to her and stuffed it down between her warm breasts.

She took it out, uncrumpled it and then glared at him again.

"Hey, this ain't what we agreed on."

"You're not worth what we agreed on," he said.

"You pay!"

"Get out!"

"Not until I get the rest of my money," she said, "You used me four times, and I gave you what you wanted."

He slapped her again and this time she staggered back a couple of steps.

"Get out, and send your pimp after me. If you do, you'll have to get a new pimp. Understand?"

"Sure," she said, "sure, I understand."

She groped behind her for the doorknob with one hand while holding her face with the other. She opened it, and ran out, leaving the door open behind her. Comfort slammed it shut and realized he had a rock-hard erection—again.

Maybe he'd chased her away too soon.

Daniels saw the girl run through the lobby as he sat in the dining room. A few minutes later he saw Comfort coming into the dining room, and some instinct told him that the girl had been running from him.

Comfort sat opposite Daniels and said, "Did you order yet?"

"No."

Comfort called the waiter over and they both ordered eggs.

"I saw a girl running from the hotel," Daniels said.

"A big girl in a cheap dress?"

"Yes."

"And you knew she was running from me, huh?"

"I guessed."

"Yeah," Comfort said, "I picked her up at a saloon last night, took her back to my room. I like big girls. This one was a little older than I usually like them, but it was late, so I settled on her."

Daniels poured himself a cup of coffee.

"Don't you want to know how she was?"

"No."

Comfort laughed.

"What did you do last night?"

"I slept."

"Alone?"

"Yes, alone."

"Too bad," Comfort said. "This city is full of women, Daniels. If I had more time last night, I could have found somebody a lot better."

"We've got other things to do, Comfort."

"I know what we have to do, Daniels."

At that moment both Williams and Samuels entered the dining room.

"Are the men all set?" Comfort asked.

"They're set boss."

Comfort looked at Daniels.

"Maybe they'll turn up today."

"They'd better," Daniels said. "If they get to a sympathetic judge—"

"Pa will take care of any judge," Comfort said.

"He doesn't own all judges, Ben," Daniels said.

"Whichever one he doesn't own now, he'll buy," Comfort said.

"What are you after, Ben?" Daniels asked. The other two men sat down, interested in the answer.

Ben Comfort looked at them and said, "Get out."

"But, boss, we haven't eaten—" Williams started.

"Get out and eat someplace else," Comfort said, "and keep checking on the men."

"Okay, boss," Samuels said, standing. He jerked his head at Williams, who also stood, and they left.

"What am I really after?" Comfort repeated. "You didn't care about your brothers, not that I could see."

"They weren't my brothers," Ben Comfort said, vehemently.

"You had the same father."

"And different mothers. After my Maw died when I was ten Pa married that . . . slut, and she gave birth to . . . to those two idiots. Believe me, I wasn't ready to share what I had with the two of them."

"So then?"

"I'm after Adams," Comfort said. "Believe me if we were only chasing that girl I'd be taking my time. She did me a favor when she killed those two morons. But Clint Adams, the Gunsmith, that's another story."

"You think you can outdraw the Gunsmith?"

"That's what I want to find out, Daniels," Comfort said. "You've seen me shoot . . ."

"In shooting contests, yes," Daniels said, "and against men who didn't stand a chance . . ."

"I never shot a man in cold blood!" Comfort cut in. "Every man I ever killed had a fair chance."

"Sure, Ben, like that farmer—"

"Never mind," Comfort said. "When we catch up with Adams, you'll find out how good I am."

Sure, Daniels said, and so will you.

TWENTY-TWO

Ellie Lennox was dressing for work when the knock came at her door. One boot on and one boot off, she limped to the door and opened it. When she saw Clint Adams standing outside she let out a whoop and threw herself into his arms. It was only then that she saw the woman who was with him.

Clint held Ellie at arms length and looked at her. She had long hair the color of a starless night, a wide mouth, full, firm breasts made to look fuller by the fact that she was not tall, perhaps five-four. She wasn't beautiful, she was pretty and she knew it. The reasons Clint liked her went much deeper than that. They had met a couple of years before, when Clint was in Denver and found himself involved in a murder. Ellie Lennox was a Pinkerton detective, and working with Clint on that murder, and solving it had gone a long way towards making Allan Pinkerton recognize her worth.*

"Hello, Ellie," he said. "You look great."

"Clint, it's good to see you," Ellie said. She looked at Katy Little Feather then and asked, "Who's your friend?"

"Meet Katy Little Feather, Ellie," Clint said. "Can we come in?"

---

*THE GUNSMITH #53.

"I'm getting ready for work," Ellie said, "but come in."

They entered and she closed the door. She and Katy both took a moment to study each other, and then Ellie said, "What can I do for you and your . . . friend?"

"I want you to set up a meeting with Allan Pinkerton for me."

"You're not one of Pinkerton's favorite people, you know?"

"I know, but I'd like you to try."

"I will. Do you want to tell me why?"

Clint looked at Katy, because the crux of the problem was hers, and she nodded. Clint explained the situation to Ellie, who pulled on her second boot while she listened. Katy watched as Ellie slipped a derringer into her boot.

When he finished his story she stood up straight and looked at both of them.

"You're expecting Pinkerton to intercede on your behalf?"

"I'd like him to act as middleman between us and the law, so we can get a fair shake."

"There's one reason why he won't do it."

"What's that?" Katy asked, speaking for the first time.

"He doesn't like Clint."

"And a reason why he will?" Katy asked.

"He's a stickler for the law," Ellie said. "If he can help you get a fair shake, I think he'll do it."

"Then you'll talk to him?" Clint asked.

"You knew I would."

"I didn't want to take it for granted."

"I appreciate that," Ellie said. "I'll talk to the old man today. Uh, how much should I tell him?"

"As much as you need to to get him to meet with me," Clint said.

"One other thing, Ellie," Clint said.

"What?"

"We worked with a lieutenant named Gorman a couple of years ago. Is he still around?"

She shook her head.

"He went east. I think he's a captain in some police force there."

"I see. Do you know anyone on the police force here?"

"I know some policemen," she said, "but Pinkerton's the one who knows the higher-ups. I'll talk to him this morning. Where can I get in touch with you?"

Without hesitation Clint told her where they were staying.

The three of them left the house together and Ellie said, "Go back to the rooming house. I'll come and see you there."

"One of us will be there," Clint said. "I want to send a telegraph message, and maybe take a look around, but one of us will be there."

"All right," Ellie said. She looked at Katy again, then at Clint and said, "I'll see you later."

Ellie walked one way and Clint and Katy went another.

"She doesn't like me," Katy said.

"When you get to know each other," Clint said, "you'll be great friends."

Shaking her head, Katy said, "Women sure like you."

"Hey," Clint said, "I have a few friends that are men, too."

"I hope you're not as close to them as you are to some of your women friends."

"Katy . . ." he said, warningly.

"I was just kidding," Katy said. "I hope Pinkerton goes for this. I don't like the idea of being on the run for the rest of my life just because some rich rancher is mad that I killed his two lowlife sons."

"If he doesn't we'll just have to do something else," Clint said.

"Like what?"

Clint hesitated a moment, then said, "We'll think of something when the time comes."

TWENTY-THREE

Seated behind his desk Allan Pinkerton listened patiently to what Ellie Lennox had to say about Clint Adams' wanting to meet with him.

"Did Adams tell you why he wanted to speak with me, Miss Lennox?"

"He did, sir."

Pinkerton waited a moment and then leaned forward and asked, "Are you prepared to tell me?"

"Only if it's absolutely necessary, sir."

"Well," Pinkerton said, sitting back again, "it is."

"Very well, sir . . ."

"You stay here," Clint said.

"Why?"

They were across the street from a telegraph office that they had located by asking someone on the street, because Clint had forgotten to ask Ellie where the nearest one was.

"Because they're looking for a man and a woman together," Clint said.

"Clint—"

"Just stay in this doorway," he said. "If anything

goes wrong, go back to the boarding house and wait for Ellie. Tell her what happened, and see if Pinkerton has agreed to be any help.''

''I want to go with you.''

''I don't want you to.''

''If something goes wrong I'll be right there,'' she said, putting her hand on her gun.

''If something goes wrong,'' he said again, very deliberately, ''get out of here.''

She stared at him, and he said, ''Katy—''

''I won't promise.''

He gave in.

''All right. Just stay here and with a little luck I'll be right back.''

He stepped out of the doorway they had been sharing and walked across the street.

Steve Connelly and Brad Armstrong saw the man crossing the street, and they saw the woman standing in the doorway across the street.

''Think it's them?'' Connelly asked.

''Man fits the description,'' Armstrong said. ''You ever seen the Gunsmith in person?''

''No, never.''

''He don't look like much, does he?''

''Nope.''

''Want to take him?''

''Nope.''

''Me neither,'' Armstrong said. ''Let's take the girl.''

''Right.''

Clint sent his telegraph message to Rick Hartman, asking for whatever he might know about Sam Comfort that might help them out of this mess.

''Will you wait for an answer, sir?''

"No," Clint said, "if an answer comes just hold onto it. Someone will be here to collect it."

"All right, sir."

Clint paid for the telegram and then left, crossing the street to the doorway where he'd left Katy Little Feather.

The doorway was empty, and there were black scuff marks on the ground.

"Damn it!"

When Connelly and Armstrong showed up at the Denver House Hotel both Comfort and Daniels were in the lobby, waiting for word from somebody.

"Is that her?" Comfort asked as the two men entered with the woman between them.

"That's her."

"Let's take her upstairs."

Up in Comfort's room they sat Katy down in a straight-backed chair, bound and gagged her, and formed a semi-circle around her.

"What about Adams?" Comfort asked.

Connelly and Armstrong exchanged glances and Daniels knew what was coming.

"Well," Connelly said, "we, uh—"

"You cowards," Comfort said. "You were afraid to take him."

"Boss, he is the Gunsmith."

"My father hired you for your guns."

"He didn't hire us to go up against no Gunsmith," Brad Armstrong said.

He and Comfort glared at each other and Daniels stepped between them.

"You boys go out and get yourselves a drink. You did all right."

Armstrong switched his gaze from Comfort to

Daniels and then, somewhat mollified by the sheriff's words, he and Connelly left.

"What do you mean they did all right?"

"What did you want them to do, get killed?" Daniels said. "If they had done that we wouldn't have the girl."

"You want the girl, Sheriff," Comfort said, "you and my father. I want Clint Adams."

"And you'll get him."

"Oh yeah? How? Now that he knows we have the girl—"

"Now that he knows that he'll come looking for her," Daniels said.

Comfort paused a moment, then said, "Yeah, but how do we find him to let him know where she is."

"We don't."

"What?"

"All we have to do is take her back to Firecreek," Daniels said. "He'll come after her."

"How's he gonna know where we took her?" Comfort demanded.

"Ben, use your head," Daniels said. "Where else would we take her?"

Ben Comfort thought about it a moment, then smiled and looked down at the woman.

"Yeah, where else?" He leaned over Katy, cupped one of her breasts in his hand and added, "And when he does come for you . . . he's a dead man!"

TWENTY-FOUR

It was all Clint could do to sit and wait at the boarding house for Ellie to show up, and he chose to do so in the living room so he'd see her as soon as she entered the house.

The landlady, Liz, found all kinds of excuses to stay around him, offering him coffee and pie, a drink. Finally she sat down on the sofa with him and stared at him.

"Where is your lady?"

"Out."

"Be out for a while?"

"I'm afraid so."

"Good," she said. "I don't like to play games, mister, so I'm gonna offer you something. If you don't want it, all you got to do is say so."

She stood up and before he could say anything she had her dress unbuttoned and her breasts were bare. They were very large and pear shaped, with rosy-colored nipples that were already incredibly distended. She cupped her breasts in her hands and flicked the nipples with her thumbs.

"I got these for you, mister, and a lot more . . . if you want it."

Clint's mouth was dry. Liz had a certain slutty quality to her that tugged at a man's insides, and her breasts were certainly desirable as he was sure the rest of her would be. How should he tell her that he would have liked to take her up on her offer but couldn't, without hurting her feelings?

Thanks but no thanks?

Any other time, but . . .

As if reading his mind she said, "Don't worry about hurting my feelings, mister. If you don't want it just say so. I don't offer it to every man I meet, but that don't mean I'm gonna die if you say no."

She lifted her breasts a little more, squeezed them and flicked the nipples again. He looked at her face and she licked her full lips. In spite of himself he had an erection. At that moment the front door opened and, to his everlasting relief, the landlady hastily tucked her proffered breasts away.

"Clint?"

He stood up and turned, and saw Ellie in the hallway.

"I see," Liz the landlady said, "you already have something extra set up," and went into the kitchen. He would have liked to explain it to her, but he didn't have time.

Ellie Lennox entered the room and said, "What was that about?"

"Never mind," Clint said. "They've got Katy."

"Who's got Katy?"

"Comfort and his posse of killers."

"How did you know?"

He explained to her what had happened at the telegraph office.

"What are you going to do?"

"Go after her."

"But you don't know where they've taken her."

"Maybe not now," he said, "but I know where they will take her."

"Where?"

"Back to Firecreek."

"To stand trial."

"Not likely," Clint said, "but I don't think they'll do anything to her until I show up."

"Alone?"

"Alone."

"Let me come with you."

"I can't, Ellie," he said. "This is for me to do, not you."

"I want to help."

"You have," he said, thinking about the landlady. "I'm going to leave right away."

He started for the stairs to go to his room and get his things and she called, "Wait."

"What?"

She moved into the hall and confronted him by the stairway.

"Pinkerton has agreed to see you."

"I can't—"

"See him before you leave, Clint," she said urgently, "then while you're gone maybe he can talk to someone for you."

"Once I get to Firecreek, Ellie, this thing is going to be settled the hard way," Clint explained. "No court, no judge and no jury."

"Talk to him, anyway," she said. "What possible harm could it do?"

Clint thought a moment then said, "Where did he agree to meet me?"

"In his office."

"When?"

"Now," she said. She approached him, and took hold of his arm. "Talk to him, Clint, and then leave."

He studied her lovely face for a moment, then put his hands on her shoulders.

"All right, Ellie. Let's go and see him."

TWENTY-FIVE

They went directly to Allan Pinkerton's office and were admitted to see him.

Pinkerton looked the same to Clint. Pink-faced, white mustache and hair, portly but powerfully built.

"Adams," Pinkerton said, with a nod.

"I appreciate your seeing me, sir," Clint said.

"Don't be subservient, Adams," Pinkerton said, "it doesn't suit you. Tell me about this problem of yours so I can be sure Miss Lennox had it all right."

Quickly, Clint explained the situation that had arisen in Firecreek, and his decision to break Katy out and take her somewhere she could tell her story.

"That means you're both wanted," he said.

"Yes," Clint replied.

"Come to the police with me, and I'll talk to them."

"Things have changed a bit in the past few hours, Mr. Pinkerton."

"Oh? How?"

He told the old man about Katy being taken back to Firecreek.

"That makes sense only if they want you as badly as they want her," Pinkerton said. "Do you know that for certain?"

"I can't know for sure," Clint said, "but a man like Comfort wouldn't dream of letting me get away with what I did."

"Hmm," Pinkerton said, stroking his mustache, "I agree with you."

"I have to go to Firecreek."

"I'd like to go with him, sir!" Ellie said quickly.

Pinkerton regarded her for a moment, then said, "I'm sure you would, Miss Lennox, but that's entirely up to him, isn't it?"

"No, Ellie."

"Clint—"

"I appreciate you seeing me, Mr. Pinkerton."

"While you're going back to Firecreek," Pinkerton said, "I'll talk to some people here. Depending on how things go there, I might be able to be of some help."

"I appreciate it."

"Clint—"

"Ellie," Clint said, "I have to go and I have to travel fast."

"You think I'd slow you down?"

"I don't know of a horse that can keep up with Duke, so yes, I think you would."

He took her by the shoulders and kissed her shortly on the mouth. Pinkerton cleared his throat and looked away.

"I'll send you a telegraph message to let you know what happens."

"And if you're dead?"

Clint shrugged and said, "Then I won't send you one."

"Go on!" she shouted. "Get out of here! Go and get killed!"

He looked at Allan Pinkerton and said, "Do me another favor?"

"What?"

"Keep her here," Clint said, and left.

"Miss Lennox."

"What?" she said, whirling on the old man.

"Can you tell me why women insist on saying things they don't mean when they're angry?"

She opened her mouth to answer, stopped to think a moment, and then said, "No, sir, I don't."

"I didn't think so," he said. "Come on."

"Where?"

"We have some people to see," he said, coming around from behind his desk, "if we're going to keep your friend from getting killed—that is, unless you really meant what you said."

"Don't be an ass," she said, and then realizing who she was talking to added very quickly, "sir."

TWENTY-SIX

Clint went to the boarding house to collect his gear, and realized that he had Katy's gear to contend with. He hated to ask the landlady to hold onto the stuff, so he took it with him to the livery.

"I have to take my horse out but I want to leave the pony and this gear with it. I'll pay you two weeks in advance."

"That's fine with me, mister. You gonna come back for it?"

"Somebody will be back for it," Clint said. "I'll saddle my horse myself."

"Whatever you say."

Clint saddled Duke and paid the man two weeks in advance. By that time everything should be resolved and somebody would return for the horse and gear.

He hoped it would be Katy herself.

Ellie Lennox went along with Pinkerton but each time he went in to speak to someone she was excluded, left outside waiting. She didn't even know who the people were he was talking to. All she knew was that they had not yet gone to the police. She only hoped that the people he had been talking to were important people.

Very important people.

Katy Little Feather felt much the same way she had when she was in a cell in Firecreek. Now she was tied to a horse being led back to Firecreek to go back into that cell, and she knew that Clint Adams would be coming after her.

This time they'd be waiting for him.

They were both as good as dead.

Ben Comfort was impatient, but he knew that this was the best way to do this. Taking the girl back to Firecreek would bring Clint Adams back there, and right into the waiting arms of Comfort.

Dan Daniels was returning to Firecreek with a totally different attitude than what he'd had when he left. He'd been intimidated by Ben Comfort because his name was Comfort. Now he knew that Comfort was not at all like his father. He was big, and brutal, but he wasn't smart, and he was fairly easy to handle.

Things were going to be different for Sheriff Dan Daniels when they got back to Firecreek.

"How far ahead of him do you think we are?" Ben Comfort asked Daniels.

"I figure with everything he's going to have to do, we should have at least a six-hour head start."

"We can widen that out by rising after dark," Comfort said.

"We don't have to do that," Daniels said.

"I *want* to do it," Comfort said. "I want to get

back in plenty of time to set up my welcome for him.''

"It doesn't matter what kind of a welcome you set up for Clint Adams," Katy said. "He'll kill you, anyway."

"You think so, huh?"

"I know so."

"You know, some of my men like you, lady," Comfort said. "They want to have a little fun with you. What do you think of that?''

"Comfort . . ." Daniels said, but he was ignored.

Katy didn't answer.

"Do you think I should let them do that?'' Comfort asked, prodding her.

"You'll let them do whatever you want, so why ask me?" Katy said.

Comfort looked at her and said, "Maybe I'm saving you for myself, whataya think of that?''

"I think I'd rather be dead," Katy said after a long moment.

Ben Comfort laughed and said, "That can be arranged too, lady.''

Dan Daniels decided that he was going to have stay close to the woman. She was technically his prisoner, and although he had no objections of holding her over for hanging, he had no desire to see her raped.

Clint left Denver knowing that he was going to have to ride Duke hard to make up some of the time Katy's abductors had on him. There was no way he was going to catch up to them, but he wanted to get to Firecreek before he was expected. To do that he might very well have to ride at night as well.

That was very probably the only chance he had of getting himself and Katy out of Firecreek alive.

TWENTY-SEVEN

The posse rode into Firecreek, Wyoming four days later. They were all dragging their butts but none more than Katy Little Feather. Each night on the trail she would stay awake as long as she could, looking for an opportunity to escape. She finally fell asleep, but so close to morning that she was awakened shortly afterward.

She was almost looking forward to being put in a cell, where she could get some sleep.

"Why are we stopping here?" Comfort asked.

"This is where the jail is," Daniels said, preparing to dismount. "That's where I'm putting her."

"No."

"No?"

"She's coming out to the ranch," Comfort said.

"Why?" Daniels asked.

"Because she's already escaped from your jail, Sheriff," Comfort said, "and when Adams gets here, I want him to come to the ranch."

"Comfort," Daniels said, "she's my prisoner—"

"No, she's not," Ben Comfort said. "She's going to be my guest at the ranch."

Katy, whose head had been hanging in exhaus-

tion, lifted her head now and looked from Daniels to
Comfort. She had an uncomfortable feeling that she
knew who was going to get their way.

Daniels stared at Comfort for a moment, then
beyond him where his men sat on their horses. They
were weary, but still ready to do as Comfort said.
There was no way Daniels could keep the girl in
town if Comfort didn't want her there.

"All right, then," Daniels said, "Then so am I."

"So are you . . . what?" Comfort asked.

"Going to be a guest at the ranch."

"But, Sheriff, you haven't been invited."

"Why don't we let your father determine that?"
Daniels suggested. "After all, it is his ranch."

Comfort regarded Daniels for a few moments,
then smiled and said, "All right, Sheriff. Let's go
talk to the old man."

They rode up to the main house of the Comfort
spread and dismounted. It was Daniels who reached
up to help Katy down from her horse.

"All right, men," Comfort said, "go and get
some rest. Williams!"

"Yeah, Boss?"

"Send me some fresh men—Gallagher, and some
of the others."

"Okay, Boss."

The front door of the house opened and the black
manservant, Rupert, stepped out. He was in his
sixties, with white hair and a pear-shaped body. He
had been with Sam Comfort for years, and had
absolutely no use for any of his sons.

"Hey, Rupert," Ben Comfort called out, "where's
the old man."

Rupert took the time to walk down the steps before answering.

"Sir, I'm afraid your father's not here."

"Where is he, then? Has he gone somewhere on business? When will he be back."

"When he left, shortly after you did, he said he was going to join the posse," Rupert said. "I expected him to return with you."

"With me?" Comfort said. "I haven't seen him since I left."

Rupert firmed up his chin and said, "I can't imagine what's become of him, then."

"Neither can I," Comfort said.

"I'll take the girl back to the jail," Daniels said.

"No," Comfort said. "Rupert will show her to a room. Rupert?"

"Is she a guest, sir?"

"She's a guest," Comfort said. "Show her to a room, and then lock her in."

"Sir?"

"Lock her in! Can't you hear, man?"

"Yes, sir."

Daniels untied Katy's hands and gave her over to Rupert.

"I'll need a room, too, Rupert," he said.

"Yes, Sheriff. How long will you be staying?"

"Until Mr. Comfort returns."

"Yes, sir. I'll prepare a room."

"Don't try to get away, lady," Comfort said as Katy went up the steps with Rupert. "There's nowhere you could run to. You're on Comfort land as far as you can see."

Katy ignored Comfort and went into the house with Rupert.

Daniels turned to Comfort and said, "I wonder what happened to your father?"

"I guess we'll just have to wait to find out."

"You're not going to go looking for him?"

Comfort stared at Daniels and said, "I just got back, Daniels. Besides, he'll be back soon enough. The old man probably got lost."

That was the second time in five minutes Daniels had heard Comfort refer to his father as an "old man," and there was nothing affectionate in the term.

Maybe Ben Comfort didn't care whether his father came back or not.

How hard would the son be to control if the father didn't return, and *he* became master?

TWENTY-EIGHT

From asking around in towns along the way Clint knew that he was only a day behind the posse. Surely they wouldn't expect him to be as close as that.

He was in a town called Benson, Wyoming in the saloon nursing a beer. He could have ridden through the night and gotten that much closer to Firecreek, but he decided instead to give Duke the rest he deserved for getting him this close.

What he had to do now was come up with some sort of plan of action. He was riding into hostile territory where the only friendly person was behind bars.

Or was she?

He had broken Katy out of the Firecreek jail once already. Would Comfort take a chance that he could do it again?

The answer was no. He was willing to bet that the Comforts would decide to keep Katy somewhere on their ranch, maybe even in the house.

That meant he could probably ride into Firecreek if he wanted, but the ranch was bound to be territory even more hostile than the town itself.

Where would the sheriff be, in town or on the ranch? He and his deputy, Zack, would recognize him as soon as he rode into town.

Who would recognize him if he rode to the ranch? Neither of the Comforts had ever laid eyes on him, though they'd surely have his description. And what about the men who had taken Katy while he'd been in the telegraph office? Surely they must have seen him, and would recognize him.

So, if neither the town nor the ranch was safe for him, where was it safe?

Nowhere near Firecreek, that was for sure, and yet that was where he had to go.

He finished his beer and stood up. He wished he had the time to sit in on a poker game that was taking place at a corner table, but he wanted to get an early start in the morning. If he pushed Duke— poor Duke—he could be near Firecreek by nightfall. Still, was there a need to push him? Wouldn't they keep Katy alive at least until he arrived? Or until they could get their bought judge back?

He had to hope that they were keeping Katy alive, whatever their reasons.

If they had killed her, they were going to have to kill him as well, because he'd see every last one of them in the ground.

Katy was in the room Rupert had taken her to. He asked her if she'd like to take a bath, and she said yes. He moved aside a partition and she saw the bathtub there. He brought water and then left her alone. She was on the second floor, and she could see that there were men on the grounds. Ben Comfort was right. Even if she did manage to get out of the house she wouldn't be able to go very far before they caught up to her. She was going to have to wait for Clint to come for her.

She undressed and eased herself into the bathtub before the water got cold. Sitting there she thought about Clint. She knew that he'd come for her. That was the kind of man he was. She also new that they'd be waiting to kill him. If he came, he'd be killed. If he didn't come, she'd be killed.

She closed her eyes and tried to make her mind a blank. She didn't want to think about what would happen if he didn't come, and she didn't want to think about what would happen if he did.

Was it selfish to hope that he would come for her and, somehow, effect both of their escapes? And if he did that, what would happen then? Would they head back to Denver again, or some-place else?

Start running again?

Like the men she had hunted down over the past few years had run, for their freedom?

She got out of the tub, dried herself off, and went to the bed. It seemed ludicrous to her that she would go to bed, to sleep, but she was tired, and when Clint came she was going to have to be in shape to . . . to run.

She got into bed and fell sleep almost imme-diately . . .

. . . and dreamt about running . . .

It was not late when Clint left the saloon, and when he noticed the telegraph office across the street he saw that it was still open. It reminded him of the telegraph message he had sent to Rick Hartman while in Denver, the one he had not gone back to get an answer for. Now, he thought of another telegraph message he could send to Rick, one he probably should have sent originally.

He crossed the street to the telegraph office and went inside.

TWENTY-NINE

Ben Comfort sat in his father's office, in his father's chair, behind his father's desk. It felt good, and why not try it out now? It was all going to be his soon.

Maybe sooner than he ever thought.

Where the hell was the old man, anyway?

At that moment the door opened and he stood up, half expecting to see his father come walking in. For a moment he felt like when he was a kid, and he'd been caught doing something he shouldn't.

But it wasn't his father, it was only Rupert.

He recognized the disapproving look on the old black man's face and very deliberately sat back down in his father's chair because he knew Rupert wouldn't like seeing him there.

"What do you want, Rupert?"

The older man stared at him for a moment, then said, "I was just checking the room while your father was gone."

"I was just trying the chair out for size," Ben said. "How does it look?"

"Only your father can fill that chair," Rupert said.

"That's what you say," Ben said, frowning. "Go on, get out of here."

"Dinner will be served in twenty minutes."

"I'll be there."

"Shall I go and bring the girl down?"

"Yeah, why don't you do that?" Comfort said. "We might as well feed her while she's . . . our guest."

"Yes, sir," Rupert said, "and the sheriff?"

"Yeah, him, too," Comfort said, easing himself back in the leather chair.

Rupert stood there a moment longer, and when Ben was about to tell him to get out the old man backed out and closed the door behind him.

The first thing Ben Comfort was going to do when he took over was fire that old black man.

Dinner was quiet.

Katy knew that Comfort and the sheriff didn't like each other, because of the way they talked to one another. Comfort felt superior to the sheriff because of who he was—or who his father was—and the sheriff seemed to tolerate Comfort.

She didn't speak because she had nothing to say.

"How do you like your room?" Ben Comfort asked.

"It's fine."

"Just fine?" he asked. "That's all? It's got to be better than anything you've ever had. You're part Indian, aren't you?"

She didn't answer.

"That room's got to be better than any tipi you've ever been in, huh?"

"Comfort . . ."

Comfort looked at the sheriff.

"What's the matter, Daniels? You want to talk to her yourself? Am I in the way?"

"Why don't you leave her alone?"

"This is my house," Comfort said. "If you don't like the way I treat my guests, why don't you just leave?"

"You'd like that, wouldn't you?" Daniels said. "You'd like me to leave her alone with you."

"Hey, Sheriff," Comfort said, "you really think I wouldn't do anything I wanted to do just because you're here?"

"She's my prisoner, Ben," Daniels said. "You're father wants her to stand trial."

"Sure, she'll stand trial," Comfort said.

"When your father gets back—"

"*If* he gets back, you mean."

"What?"

"What if he doesn't come back, did you ever think of that? What if he's dead?"

"I don't—"

"If he never comes back all of this is mine—the house, the ranch, the town, the power!"

"You think your father's power comes from what he owns?"

"Power comes from money," Ben Comfort said, "and I'll have that, too."

"You'll have your father's money," Daniels said, "and you'll have his house, and his land, but you'll never have his power, because his power comes from who he is."

Ben Comfort slammed his hand down on the table, upsetting his plate, and stood up.

"You don't think I could have my own power?" he bellowed.

"I don't," Katy said.

Comfort glared at her.

"I don't either," Daniels said.

Comfort looked as if he were ready to explode, but suddenly be brought himself under control and smiled at them both.

"I'll show you both that you're wrong," he said, and left the dining room.

Katy looked at Daniels and decided to take advantage of Ben Comfort's absence.

"I don't suppose there's any chance that you'll let me go."

Daniels looked at her and smiled.

"You know I can't do that."

"He's going to kill me, you know?" she said. "He's crazy."

"You're going to stand trial."

"You're a fool if you believe that."

Daniels looked at her and said, "I'm no fool, but maybe I don't believe it."

"You're the law in Firecreek, Sheriff," she said. "You know I shouldn't be here, I should be in jail."

"It'll all work out," Daniels said, pouring himself a glass of wine. Hopefully, he added to himself, it would all work out to his own benefit.

"Not in my favor, I'm afraid," she said. "He's coming for me, you know."

"Adams," Daniels said, nodding. "I know."

"Somebody's going to get killed," Katy said. "Maybe a lot of people."

"I know."

"What are you going to do about it?"

"I'm going to do what will do me the most good," Sheriff Dan Daniels said.

"And what's that?"

"Wait and pick up the pieces."

THIRTY

Katy had come to think of the room she was in as "her" room. It was better than thinking of it as her prison. Besides, the room was nothing like the cell she had been in before, and for that she was grateful. She seemed to have more optimism being held in the house than she'd had when she was in the cell, in spite of the fact that the odds were certainly stacked against both she and Clint as far as getting out of this alive.

She was back in her room after dinner, contemplating whether to ask Rupert if she could have another bath when there was a knock at the door. That didn't surprise her, because when Rupert had come to tell her that dinner was ready he had knocked.

She opened the door, expecting to see Rupert, and instead it was Ben Comfort.

"Hello, lady."

"What do you want?"

"I came up to have a talk," he said. She could smell the whiskey on him, and knew that he had been drinking heavily since dinner.

"You're drunk."

"You're damn right I'm drunk," he said, weaving towards her. She backed away and he stepped into the room. She realized that, even drunk, he had just outmaneuvered her.

He closed the door behind him and faced her.

"Get out or I'll scream."

He laughed.

"Scream all you want. This is my house."

"What do you want, Comfort?"

"I told you," he said, "I just want to talk."

"About what?"

"About you," he said. "About you getting away from here alive."

"You want to help me get away?"

"Sure," he said, amiably, "why not? All you did was get rid of two thorns in my side."

"When will you let me go?"

"Well," Comfort said, "if the old man doesn't come back soon, I'll have no reason to hold you."

"Are you telling me—"

"That is," Comfort said, "unless I want to."

"What do you mean?"

"I may want to keep you here and watch you stand trial," he said.

"I don't understand."

"Well," he said, "if you made it worth my while, I'd be more willing to let you go."

"Worth your while?"

"Come on, lady," Comfort said, moving closer to her, "you know what I mean."

She did know what he meant, and she wasn't willing to go to bed with him, not even to save her life—at least, not while there was a chance that she could still escape.

"Get out!"

He frowned.

"Too good for me, huh?"

"You're a pig!"

He slapped her then and she staggered back. The back of her knees struck the bed and she fell onto it in a seated position.

"Take off your clothes," he said.

"No."

"Oh," he said, "I get it. You want to see what you're in for. All right . . ."

She watched in horror as he began to undress. He pulled his boots off, almost falling as he drunkenly balanced himself, then took off his shirt and pants. He must have prepared for this beforehand because he wore no underwear. His erection popped into view as soon as he dropped his pants, swollen and heavily veined. It was easily the ugliest penis she'd ever seen.

"There you go, lady," he said, grabbing hold of his cock with his right hand and waving it at her. "It's all yours."

"You're disgusting," she said. She looked around for a place to run, but there was nowhere to go but past him, and even in his drunken state she didn't think she'd be able to accomplish that. She started looking for something to use as a weapon."

"I'm gonna have to use force, huh?" he said. "Well, that's all right. I've done that before."

"You brag about raping women?"

"No woman ever gets raped, lady," he said. "They all want it, some just want it harder than others."

"Well," she said, "I don't want it at all," and with that she kicked out at him. She had hoped to catch him in the balls, but he turned and took the kick on one muscular thigh.

"Didn't think I'd be ready for that, did you?" he said, laughing. "Come here!"

He reached out for her and grabbed her by the front of her shirt. She resisted and when he pulled harder the buttons of the shirt gave and her breasts bobbed into view.

"All right," he said, eyeing her breasts hungrily. He pulled at the shirt, tearing it off her completely so that she was naked to the waist.

"Come on," he said, "you know you want it."

"Get away from me" she said, but he grabbed her by both breasts and squeezed. She cried out in pain, trying to pull away, but he was too powerful. He squeezed harder and she screamed.

He pushed her then, and she fell onto the bed on her back. He pounced on her, pinning her with his weight. Holding her down he slid further up so that he was sitting on her chest. He leaned forward so that his penis rested between her breasts, the swollen head even with her chin.

"Open wide, bitch!" he said, and inched further up.

Just then the door opened violently. She didn't see it, but she heard it slam into the wall as it flew open. Looking up, she saw an arm slide beneath Ben Comfort's chin and pull the man's head back. Comfort had no choice but to go with the pressure or risk a broken neck.

She thought it was going to be Clint, but as Comfort moved off her and she propped herself up, she saw that it was Sheriff Dan Daniels.

Daniels spun Comfort around and then released him. Drunkenly, Comfort kept going until he hit the wall and slid down to a seated position.

"Get out, Ben!" Daniels said.

"What do you th—think you're doing?" Comfort demanded, staggering back to his feet.

"Take your clothes and get."

"This is my house . . ."

"And this is my prisoner!" Daniels said. "No matter what you say, Ben, I'm taking her back to town with me tomorrow and putting her in a cell, where she should be."

Comfort looked at Katy, then he looked at Daniels and said, "I get it. You want her for yourself."

"You're drunk, Ben," Daniels said. "Go to bed and sleep it off."

"I'll go to bed," Comfort said, moving towards the door with his clothes in his arms. "We'll settle this tomorrow, Sheriff."

"At least then you'll be sober."

Comfort left the room and Daniels slammed the door behind him.

He turned to look at Katy, who had stood up. When his eyes fell on her breasts, he stared for a moment, then hurriedly looked away.

"I'm sorry that happened," he said. "If I had taken you to the jail, it wouldn't have."

"It's not your fault," Katy said. She made no move to hide her breasts. Where she wouldn't have slept with Comfort to save her life, she made the immediate decision to sleep with the sheriff— if he'd have her—to try and get him to help her escape.

He looked at her again, at her firm, dark tipped breasts, then said, "You'd better get some sleep. We'll be going to town in the morning."

"All right," she said.

The sheriff moved towards the door and she said, "Sheriff?"

"What?"

"He might come back." She wondered if he'd seen that as enough of an invitation.

"He won't," Daniels said, "but if it will make you feel better I'll sit outside your door."

"I'd be happier if you sat inside my door," she said. Surely, he'd see that as an invitation.

He turned and stared at her now, boldly studying her. She straightened her back to jut her breasts and stared back at him.

"Hell," he said softly.

He turned and walked out the door.

When Katy went to bed she couldn't sleep. For some reason she couldn't understand, she was sexually excited. Was she one of those women who liked violent sex, like Comfort had said? She didn't think so. She thought that maybe it had more to do with the fact that she didn't know what was going to happen to her the next day, and the fact that Sheriff Daniels was sitting outside her door, and was not an unattractive man.

If she was going to die tomorrow, she wouldn't have minded having sex tonight.

Dan Daniels couldn't sit still.

He'd taken a straight-backed chair from his room and positioned it in front of Katy's room, and then sat in it. He'd slept in a chair many times over the years, but tonight he couldn't. He had to keep shifting to accommodate the erection he had. Ever since he'd seen Katy Little Feather naked to the waist, her breasts heaving as she caught her breath after wrestling with Comfort, he'd had an erection that just wouldn't go away.

He knew she had invited him to stay with her—

twice. He also knew what her reasons had to be, but he still cursed himself for walking out instead of taking her up on her offer. How many times does a beautiful woman offer herself to you, for whatever reason?

He shifted again, adjusting his penis to a more comfortable position, when the door to the room opened behind him.

He jumped up from his seat and turned and saw Katy Little Feather standing in the doorway—completely naked, this time.

"I know what you're up to, you know?" he said.

"Do you?"

"You think if I sleep with you I'll let you go in the morning."

"The thought had crossed my mind," she said.

He was surprised by her honesty.

"And if I do sleep with you," he said, "and don't let you go?"

"Then we had an enjoyable night," she said, with a shrug, "and I go to jail."

He stared at her for a few moments—her breasts, her flat stomach and wide hips, her lovely thighs and legs, and the black patch of hair between her legs.

"Hell," he said, and moved the chair out of the way.

THIRTY-ONE

Dan Daniels woke the next morning with doubts. The night he had spent with Katy Little Feather had been the most satisfying of his life. He did not have a lot of experience with women, but of the women he had spent such time with, none had compared to Katy.

He wasn't naive enough to think that Katy had slept with him for any reason other than to try and convince him to let her go. On the other hand, he thought he was smart enough to realize that she had also enjoyed their night together.

If her aim had indeed been to convince him to let her go free, then she had succeeded.

He was convinced!

Clint rode into Firecreek that morning, aware that there were two men who definitely knew him by sight, Sheriff Daniels and the deputy, Zack. Instead of riding down the main street he approached the town from behind the livery stable and entered the stable by the back door.

"S'posed to come in the front," the liveryman said.

"I got lost," Clint said. "Cool him down and feed him lightly."

"He looks hungry."

"He is, but I may need him again . . . soon."

The man shrugged and said, "He's your horse."

"I also want to leave my gear here."

"Cost you extra."

"What a surprise," Clint said, paying the man. "Don't hide the stuff."

"I know. You may need it fast. You gonna rob the bank?"

"Is it worth robbing?"

"Not for what I got in it," the man said, and led Duke away.

Clint made his way cautiously down the street to the sheriff's office. He wanted to determine whether Daniels had taken Katy out to the Comfort ranch, or had locked her in a cell.

In front of the office he stopped to look in the window. The deputy was inside, in a familiar position. He had both feet up on the desk and was leaning back in his chair.

Clint turned the doorknob quietly and entered quickly and silently.

Before the deputy knew it, Clint was standing on the other side of the desk.

"Jesus!" Zack said, dropping his feet.

"Put your feet back on the desk!" Clint commanded, and the deputy complied immediately.

"Uh, are you here to give up?"

"No," Clint said, "I'm here to see the sheriff."

"To give up?"

"Is he here?"

"He ain't, and that's a fact," Zack said. "Fact is, I ain't seen him since he left with the posse, and most of them came back." Zack narrowed his eyes suddenly and asked, "Did you kill him?"

"I didn't kill anyone," Clint said. "If he's not here that means he took the girl out to the ranch."

"Girl? What girl?" Zack asked, looking confused.

"Never mind," Clint said. "Get up."

"You told me—"

"Now I'm telling you to get up!" Clint snapped.

"Yessir." The deputy stood up quickly.

"Take your gun out of your holster and put it in a desk drawer."

The deputy obeyed.

"Let's go to a cell. Where are the keys?"

The deputy opened a drawer—a different one from where he had just placed his gun—and took out a key ring.

"Give it here."

He tossed it to Clint.

"Move."

They walked to the back where Clint locked the man in a cell.

"You're nice and safe in here, Deputy," Clint said. "Take my advice. Don't call for help. Stay in here where it's safe. Somebody will let you out tonight."

"Yessir," the deputy said.

"Do what you're good at," Clint said. "Take a nap."

Clint went back into the office and locked the front door. In the back Zack stared at the bars for a few seconds, then shrugged, laid down on the cot and took a nap.

Katy woke while the sheriff was getting dressed.

"Leaving?" she asked.

"I . . . have to," Daniels said awkwardly.

"I understand."

"I've got to talk to Ben."

She propped her head on her hand and said nothing.

He finished dressing and then looked at her. Hair tousled and eyes puffy from sleep—or lack of it— she was still incredibly lovely.

"Don't you want to know what I'm going to do?"

"Sure I do."

"But you didn't ask."

"I don't want to push you, Dan," Katy said.

"Jesus," Daniels said, "you're really something."

"You do what you have to do," Katy said. "I'll understand."

"You're too damned understanding, if you ask me."

"Would you like it better if I badgered you?"

"Maybe," he said. "I don't know."

"Well, I'll tell you anyway," he said. "I'm going to let you go."

"You'll get yourself in trouble."

"I'm not worried about that," he said.

"I am."

"Jesus, would you show a little self-interest here?" he said, exasperated.

"I am, Dan," she said. "I don't want you to let me go. That's not what I'm after."

"Then what are you after?"

"I want my name cleared," she said. "I don't want to be on the run for the rest of my life for something I didn't do."

"You killed those boys," the sheriff pointed out.

"I killed two men," she said, "who were wanted for murder, and I did not kill them in cold blood. Everyone who was in that saloon knows that."

"None of them will come forward," Daniels said. "They're afraid of the Comforts."

"Has the father returned, I wonder?" she said.

"That's something else I want to find out," he said. "What happened to him?"

"With him not around can you control Ben Comfort?"

"I don't know," he said. "Ben's a dangerous man. He's good with a gun, and I'm not. If I'm going to control him I've got to outsmart him. I can't match him man to man."

He seemed embarrassed to admit that.

"Yes you can," she said. "Maybe not physically, but I'd put my money on you."

Daniels stared at her and his mind was a confused jumble of emotions. He was amazed at how quickly their relationship had changed from captor and captive to . . . to what?

"It's still early," he said. "Get some sleep. I'll talk to you later."

"All right."

Daniels went to the door, hesitated, then grabbed the knob and turned it savagely.

Outside the door he stood still for a moment, trying to regain his composure, and then went downstairs to find Ben Comfort.

Katy Little Feather felt almost as much confusion as Dan Daniels did. She had never expected this when he first arrested her, and she didn't quite know what was going to happen in the end. She hated the thought that she had used her body to get Daniels to help her, but on the other hand she had enjoyed their night together.

Her future was just as clouded as before, and a little more complicated.

THIRTY-TWO

Clint waited in the sheriff's office.

He decided that it would be better if he would approach the Comfort ranch at night, after dark. He knew he was taking a chance with Katy's life by waiting, but he'd be taking an even bigger chance with both their lives if he rode out there in broad daylight.

He was taking another chance by using the sheriff's office to wait in. He had drawn the curtains over the windows and locked the door. Once or twice someone had tried to enter, but they had given up after finding the door locked. He hoped they would just assume that Deputy Zack was goofing off.

There hadn't been a word out of Zack all morning, and the one time Clint had checked on him the man had been sleeping peacefully in his cell.

He could have left the office, but there was always the chance that the sheriff would ride into town and spot him, or maybe one of the men from the posse who might have seen him in Denver.

He was playing it very safe because he knew there was only going to be one chance for him to go in, get Katy and get them both out again.

Alive.

• • •

Katy stayed in her room all morning. She had no
choice because the door was locked, but she would
have stayed there, anyway, waiting for Daniels to
come back with some news.

She stood by the window looking out, and saw
that Comfort had men actually patrolling the grounds.
If the sheriff could get her out before Clint came,
maybe she could intercept Clint and keep him from
walking into a trap.

If the sheriff could get her out at all.

"Why don't you come into the office, Sheriff?"
Comfort said. "We can discuss it there."

"There's nothing to discuss, Comfort," Daniels
said. "I'm taking her to town—now!"

Comfort stared at Daniels and said calmly, "There's
something in the office that might change your mind."

"What?"

"Come with me."

"Has your father returned?"

Comfort didn't answer, he simply started walking
towards the office. Finally, Daniels followed.

Comfort opened the door and went inside, leaving
the door open. Daniels went in behind him.

"What's going—" he started to say, but the door
slammed shut behind him and he turned and found
himself looking down the barrels of two guns.

"Take his gun," Comfort said, and one of the
men did so, sliding it out of Daniels' holster and
tucking it into his own belt.

"What's going on here, Comfort?" Daniels demanded.

Standing behind his father's desk, Ben Comfort
straightened to his full height.

"You think I don't know what's going on?" he

demanded. "You crawled into that squaw's bed, and now you want to take her to town?"

"I planned to take her to town last night," Daniels said. "You know that."

"Sure, but after spending the night with her your plan now is to take her to town and let her go . . . isn't that right?"

The guilt was evident on Daniels' face and Comfort saw it with great satisfaction.

"Yeah, well," he said, "plans have changed . . . Sheriff." He looked past Daniels at his men and said, "Put him away." He dropped his eyes down to the top of the desk, as if there were something there of great interest.

"What are you going to do?"

Slowly, Comfort raised his eyes to look at Sheriff Daniels.

"We're gonna put you in a room for a while, Sheriff," he said. "Hey, maybe we'll even put you next to your girlfriend."

"When your father returns—"

"Hell, he's got until tonight to do that, and then I'm taking over," Comfort said. "Tomorrow, we'll have a little trial of our own. Maybe we'll even make you a defendant. What do you think of that?"

"You're crazy, Comfort."

"Maybe," Comfort said, "but I'm in control here, Sheriff. Total control." He looked at his men, waved his hand and said, "Take him."

Daniels felt a surge of helplessness as each man took hold of an arm and propelled him out the door and up to the second floor.

He'd failed Katy, and he'd failed himself.

He recognized now that the only chance Katy had, the only chance *he* had was Clint Adams.

What a difference a day makes.

Katy became aware of the commotion out in the hall and ran to put her ear to the door. She heard the sound of footsteps, some voices she couldn't quite make out, and then the slamming of a door.

She was afraid she knew what that meant.

Suddenly, a key slid into the lock on her door and she backed from it, hoping against hope that Sheriff Dan Daniels would enter the room.

The door opened, and Ben Comfort walked in, smiling.

As they pushed Daniels into the room next to Katy's, one of the men struck him on the back of the head with his gun, knocking him to the floor. He didn't lose consciousness, but he lay on his face for a few moments, waiting for the pain of dizziness to pass.

"Hello, lady," Comfort said.

"What's going on?" she asked. "What happened?"

"Oh, nothing much. I've just had your new boyfriend put in the room next to you."

"What did you do to him?"

"Nothing," Comfort said. "All I did was show who was in charge here, once and for all."

"Did you hurt him?"

Comfort didn't answer. Instead he said, "How do you think Adams will feel when he finds out you let Daniels into your bed?"

"Did you hurt him?"

"He is coming for you, isn't he?" Comfort asked

her. "Of course, he is. The great Gunsmith will be here shortly and I'll have both of your boyfriends right where I want them," he said, "in the palm of my hand."

He showed her his palm, and then he moved closer to her and touched her hair before she had a chance to pull away from him.

"Maybe then I can be your new boyfriend, huh?"

"I'd rather be dead."

She thought he was going to hit her, but he smiled and just chucked her under the chin.

"That can be arranged, too."

"I have a trial coming."

"And you'll get it," he said, backing away from her. "In the morning, right after breakfast."

"What? You can't do—" Katy started to complain, but Comfort backed out of the room, closed the door and locked it.

The sound of the key turning in the door suddenly sounded like the key turning in a cell door.

THIRTY-THREE

Dan Daniels rolled over and sat up. The back of his head hurt, but he felt capable of standing now. He did so, staggering a little but keeping his feet.

He knew he was in the room next to Katy's, but there wasn't much he could do for her, or for himself. He was fairly certain that Comfort would leave a man outside his door.

He looked out the window. The grounds were being patrolled. They were waiting for Adams to show up. Adams had one thing working in his favor, and that was that the men outside probably had been told not to kill him. Comfort wanted to save that pleasure for himself.

It was the only thing Adams had working for him, unless he did the smart thing and just didn't show up.

Comfort was in the office—his office, now—sitting behind his desk. He felt certain that Adams would be there by the next day, and he had his men ready and waiting, with instructions not to kill him.

He was going to get to face the Gunsmith, and he'd have plenty of witnesses when he killed him.

With his father's wealth and position, and the

Gunsmith's reputation, there would be no stopping him from getting everything he wanted—whatever that was.

He'd figure that out after this was all over.

The afternoon wore on into early evening. Clint moved to the window and carefully looked outside. Everything was going on normally out there. It was easy to imagine that someone knew he was inside and was waiting for him to come out, but he knew that wasn't the case. He was still safe in the office—a safety he would soon have to leave.

Even though he knew that Comfort and his men would be waiting for him, he felt he had one thing in his favor. They'd be expecting him tomorrow, probably late tomorrow. By appearing tonight, he had the element of surprise on his side—as much as he could, with a ranch full of armed men just waiting for him.

His intent was to wait until about an hour before dark, and then leave the office and fetch Duke from the livery. By the time he approached the ranch it would be almost totally dark.

He turned and walked back to the sheriff's desk and sat down behind it. He took out the telegram he'd finally received in Benson from Rick Hartman and read it again.

Maybe it would be his final ace in the hole.

As early evening approached Katy found herself sitting at the window looking out. She was waiting for Clint to walk into this trap and get her out of here. She felt selfish. What would she do if Clint did get in and free her? Would he also free Sheriff

Daniels on her word? Would she even ask him to do
that? If she did, she'd have to explain why.

She remembered Comfort asking her what Clint
would think when he found out that she had slept
with Sheriff Daniels. It wouldn't bother Clint anymore than it bothered her to know that he had slept
with Anne Archer, and Sandy Spillane, and probably
with that lady detective from Denver, Ellie Lennox—
and many other women. She and Clint were friends,
and that was all.

She and Daniels weren't even that—yet. Would
she risk herself and Clint by asking Clint to also free
Daniels?

She covered her face with both hands. This was
crazy thinking. How was Clint going to get through
the patrols that had been sent out onto the grounds?

She couldn't just sit here anymore.

She had to do something!

THIRTY-FOUR

"Stay on your toes," one man said.

"Why?" the second man said. "He's not due until tomorrow."

"That's why you should keep your eyes open," the first man said.

Clint watched as the first man rode away and the second man wheeled his horse around. He was close enough to have heard their conversation, and had gotten that close on foot. He had left Duke a few hundred yards away, not at all concerned that the big gelding might make some noise.

He was afraid for a moment that the second man was going to ride away, but he paused to roll himself a cigarette. That gave the first man time to get far enough away that he wouldn't hear the commotion.

Clint moved out from behind the stand of brush he was using as cover. As the man was getting ready to light his cigarette, Clint grabbed his arm and pulled him off his horse. He hit the ground hard, the word "Hey" jarred from him, but before he could say anything more Clint hit him twice. He then rolled the unconscious man over, took the rope off the man's horse and trussed him up with it. He took the reins of the man's horse and tied him to the same stand of brush he'd used as cover. He didn't want the riderless animal going "home" to the ranch and giving him away.

Clint wondered how many men the Comforts had on patrol out here, but he was willing to bet that most of the armed men would be patrolling an area around the house. They wanted to keep Katy in as badly as they wanted to keep him out.

That is, if they wanted to keep him out.

There was another way to look at this. Maybe they were keeping most of the men close to the house because they wanted him to get at least that far. If they were really intent on keeping him away from the house, then he wouldn't have been able to get this far inside Comfort land so easily.

They were defending the ranch against him.

They were waiting for him.

With that in mind he moved in the direction of the house, the lights of which he could see from where he was. Katy was in there, and he had to try and get her out. The fact that they were awaiting him would just make it a little harder.

All right, it would make it a *lot* harder.

Katy gave up.

She had been trying to find something to pry the door of her room off its hinges, but she finally abandoned that foolishness. With the sheriff in the next room there was bound to be a man in the hall.

Yes, that was it.

A *man* in the hall.

She walked to the dresser and picked up the water pitcher and placed it on the little table by the bed. Then she went to the door and began to pound on it.

"Hey! You out there!" She only hoped that Comfort wouldn't hear the commotion.

She heard footsteps move towards her door.

"Hey! Come on!"

There was a moment of absolute silence and then a voice said from the hall, "What do you want?"

"Open the door," she said, unbuttoning her shirt.

"What for?"

"I want to show you something."

She removed her shirt, leaving herself naked to the waist.

"I-I'm, not supposed to—"

"Come on," she said, "I need you."

"What?"

"I need you!"

She wet the fingers of both hands with her tongue and then used her fingers to wet her nipples. When they didn't stiffen right away from the chill she tweaked them until they did stiffen.

She heard a key being slipped into the lock and stepped away from the door. She wanted the man to see her as soon as he opened the door.

As the door opened she straightened her back and pushed her breasts forward. When the man stepped in, gun in hand, he stopped short at the sight of her nakedness and his jaw dropped.

"Close the door," she said hurriedly.

"What?"

"The door! Close it!"

Still numb, he obeyed.

"I need a man," she said.

"Huh?"

"A man," she said, cupping her breasts and lifting them. "I need a man. You're a man, aren't you?"

"Uh, yeah . . ."

"Come on," she said. She undid her pants and slid them down over her hips slowly until they were pooled at her feet. She stepped from them and kicked them away, and then removed her panties. When she was totally nude she sat on the bed and then moved herself back onto it, until she was leaning on the pillows

"Please," she said, spreading her legs, "I need you."

The man, a young man with jug ears and a long jaw, finally realized what was going on. He licked his lips and holstered his gun, then moved towards the bed.

"Get undressed," she said. "I want to see you."

She could see the bulge in the front of his pants as he moved around the side of the bed.

"I'm not supposed to be in here," he said.

She could reach him now and took his hand to press it to her breast.

"I won't tell," she whispered, "I promise."

She rubbed his palm over her nipple and suddenly he pulled his hand away. She thought that maybe she had lost him, but he simply wanted to use both hands to get undressed.

He undid his gun belt and let it fall to the floor, and then started to take off one boot. He lifted his right foot with his hands, leaving himself fighting for balance on his left.

"Oh, yes," she said, reaching out to touch his crotch.

"God," he said, "you really want it, don't you?"

"Yes," she said, "I really do."

She closed her hand over his balls, squeezing them as hard as she could right through the pants, and his eyes bulged. He opened his mouth to cry out but she grabbed the water pitcher with the other hand and cracked him over the head with it.

He staggered, fought for balance, and then fell. She was off the bed like a cat, swinging the pitcher again. He brought one arm up to defend himself, but he didn't have full possession of his senses. She was easily able to club him again, and he keeled over, unconscious.

She put the pitcher down and searched his pockets for the keys. After she pulled on her pants, she hurried from the room and down the hall and began to try keys in the lock of the room where Daniels was being held.

"Who's there?" she heard Daniels call from inside.

"Shhh," she said. "Quiet."

"Katy? Is that you?"

"Shut up!" she hissed, trying key after key. The man had a huge ring of keys, probably one for every room in the house, and then some.

She kept looking down the hall, expecting to see Ben Comfort any minute. Finally, one of the keys fit and she unlocked the door.

As it opened Daniels took one look at her and said, "What the hell—"

She was still naked to the waist, and seemed to just notice it, herself.

"Come on to my room," she said, "and close the door."

She hurried to her own room, followed closely by Daniels. When he entered, he saw the man on the floor and was quick enough to figure out what had happened.

He turned to Katy and saw her buttoning her shirt.

"His gun," he said.

"There," she said, inclining her head towards it.

Daniels picked up the gun belt and strapped it on.

"We've got to get out of here," he said.

"I agree completely," she said, smiling. "Let's go."

On foot, Clint was within spitting distance of the house. That he had been able to get this far without encountering anyone other than the one sentry further supported his theory that they *wanted* him to.

He looked up at the house and wondered which of the windows was the room Katy was being held in.

Suddenly, he heard a very familiar sound—the sound of the hammer being cocked on a gun, but magnified tenfold. He turned and found himself looking at a group of men, fanned out and all holding guns on him. One man stepped from behind them and confronted him.

"Clint Adams?"

"That's right."

"The Gunsmith?"

Clint didn't answer.

The man smiled and said, "Yeah, you're the Gunsmith, all right."

"What of it?"

"I've been waiting for you."

"I know."

The man frowned.

"What do you mean, you know?"

"I certainly wouldn't have been able to get this far if you hadn't been expecting me, would I?"

"You knew that and you came, anyway?"

Now Clint smiled, hoping to throw the man—who had to be Ben Comfort—off balance.

"You don't think I came alone, do you?"

Suddenly, Comfort grew edgy and looked around him.

"Get his gun and bring him inside!" he ordered, and stalked towards the house.

Two men broke from the group and approached him. Clint backed off a step, turning his gun side away from them.

"Be nice, Adams," one of them said. "Don't die before your time."

"I could give you the same advice," Clint said, but he allowed his gun to be taken from him.

"Let's go inside," the man who disarmed him said. "Maybe the boss will let you have a drink . . . first."

"I'd prefer to have a drink," Clint said, "after."

THIRTY-FIVE

Daniels and Katy were working their way down the hall, Daniels with gun in hand, Katy close behind. When they reached the head of the steps, the front door opened and they moved back.

Daniels peered around and saw Ben Comfort enter. His shoulders were stiff and his stride purposeful. He had left the door open so Daniels waited and watched.

"What—" Katy started to ask, but he stopped her with a hand gesture. Impatient, she pushed close to him and peered downstairs on her own. They both saw a group of men enter, and they both saw that Clint Adams was in their midst.

"Oh, no," she breathed.

Daniels pushed her back and backed up himself, so that they were both in the hall.

"We have to help him," she said.

"We'll have enough trouble helping ourselves," he pointed out.

"He came here to help me," she said. "I can't leave him."

Daniels thought about it for a moment. Katy misinterpreted his silence.

173

"Give me the gun then," she said, reaching for it.

"Wait a minute," he said. "I didn't say I wouldn't help him, but let's wait and see what happens."

"Comfort is going to kill him, that's what's going to happen."

"No," Daniels said, "at least, he's not going to kill him in cold blood."

"How do you know?"

"Because Adams is the Gunsmith," Daniels said, "and Comfort wants to try him."

"He has to give him a gun for that."

"He will," Daniels said, "and I'm sure he'll have a dozen of his men around them. At the first indication that Adams will win . . ." he said, and let his voice trail off.

"They'll kill him."

"I'm afraid so."

"We have to do something."

"Yes, we do," he said. "We have to find some more guns."

Clint was ushered into an office where the man he took to be Ben Comfort was standing behind a desk. All of the men he had with him outside crowded into the room, and Clint was able to count nine, including Comfort.

"Ben Comfort, I presume," Clint said.

"That's right, Adams," Comfort said. "You've heard of me?"

"No."

Comfort frowned. He didn't like the answer.

"Well, after tonight a lot of people are going to hear of me."

"Oh? Why is that?"

"Because this is the night I'm going to kill the Gunsmith."

Clint waited a few moments, looked around the room at all of the other men and asked Comfort, "Are you going to pull the trigger yourself?"

A couple of men snickered but Comfort's quick look quieted them.

"You bet I'm going to pull the trigger," Comfort said. "It's going to be a fair fight, Adams."

Comfort turned his attention to one of his men and said, "Stephens, take some men and take a look around outside."

Stephens picked out five men and they all went outside.

"Don't think I believe that you didn't come here alone, Adams," Comfort said. "I'm just playing it safe."

"Sure, Comfort. Tell me, where is this big show-down between us going to take place? In the dark?"

Comfort smiled and said, "Don't worry. There'll be plenty of light so that you can see the bullet coming."

"Is your father going to watch?"

"My father," Comfort said, "has conveniently pulled a disappearing act."

"Convenient for who?"

"For me, of course," Ben Comfort said. "I'm in power here now. If I'm real lucky, the old man will never come back."

"Aren't you curious about what happened to him?"

"I couldn't care less," Comfort said, and Clint believed him.

There went his ace in the hole.

While Clint, Comfort and the other men were in the office, Daniels and Katy made their way down the steps.

"Where?" Katy whispered.

Daniels motioned for her to follow him and they left the entry hall for another part of the house.

He led her past the dining room into another room. The walls of the room were covered with guns, both handguns and rifles.

"Take your pick," he said. "Get me a Winchester. I'll watch the door."

Quickly she took two Winchesters from the wall and a Colt from a display case. She found ammunition for all the weapons, loaded them and put extra shells into her pockets. She joined Daniels at the door and handed him a rifle. He holstered his handgun and accepted the Winchester.

"Now what?" she asked.

"We've got to figure out where they're going to set this up," he said. "It can't be outside. It's too dark."

"They could light torches."

He shook his head.

"It would take too long—but maybe not in a more confined area."

"Like where?"

He looked at her and said, "Like the stable."

THIRTY-SIX

"One of your men said something about a drink," Clint said to Comfort.

Comfort said to one of his men, "Get the man a drink, Corey."

While the man was pouring a drink Comfort turned and looked out the window.

"Forget it, Comfort," Clint said.

Comfort looked at Clint over his shoulder and said, "Forget what?"

Clint accepted a glass of very expensive brandy and said, "I lied."

"About what?"

"About not coming alone."

"You mean, you did come alone?"

"That's right."

"Even though you knew we were waiting?"

"That's right."

Clint sipped the brandy. It was very good. He wondered how long it would take Ben Comfort to go through his father's supply.

"That's crazy," Comfort said, turning to face Clint. "Does the woman mean that much to you?"

"She's my friend," Clint said. "I try to take care of my friends."

"Your friend?" Comfort said. "Your friend was in bed with the sheriff last night. What do you think of that?"

"That's her choice," Clint said.

"You don't care?"

"Not a bit. Why should I?"

"I thought—"

"You thought wrong," Clint said, "and you're thinking wrong if you think I'm going to let you kill me."

Comfort straightened up and hooked his thumbs into his gun belt.

"You ain't gonna have a choice, Adams. I'm gonna kill you because I'm faster."

"And if I'm faster," Clint said, "your men will kill me, right?"

"They won't interfere."

Clint smiled and said, "You're a bad liar."

Comfort opened his mouth to respond, but the office door opened and Stephens walked back in.

"Well?" Comfort asked.

"Nothing," Stephens said, "he came alone."

"I told you."

"Yeah," Comfort said, "you told me."

It was clear that the man had his doubts now. Why would Clint admit that he had come alone?

Unless he didn't.

"Is everything ready?" Comfort asked Stephens.

"All set, boss."

"All right, then," Comfort said. He looked at Clint and said, "Let's go." He still had a slight frown on his face.

Comfort was a little confused at the moment, and that was what Clint wanted.

•   •   •

Daniels and Katy had successfully made their way to the stable. They entered by a back door and once inside they split up.

"If we're right, we're going to have to have a tactical advantage," Daniels said.

"A crossfire."

"Right."

"We'll have to go up top."

"Let's wait until our eyes adjust to the darkness," Daniels said. "We don't need to break a leg in the dark."

They stood there together, listening to each other's breathing, and abruptly Katy stood on her toes and kissed him on the mouth.

"What's that for?" he asked.

"For agreeing to help my friend."

"Your friend?" he said. "Is that all Clint Adams is to you?"

"Yes," she said, "a very good friend."

Daniels hesitated a moment, then said, "All right. Let's go."

"Good luck," she said, and melted into the darkness.

THIRTY-SEVEN

Comfort and his men walked Clint over to the stable. A couple of men went in ahead of them and Clint could see that they were lighting lamps inside.

"Inside," Comfort said, pushing Clint from behind.

Inside they had set enough lamps up so that it almost looked like daylight. The door closed behind him and he was alone with nine armed men, all of whom would have killed him for two bits.

Ben Comfort, on the other hand, was ready to do it for free.

"All right," Comfort said, "gather round, boys."

His men formed a line on each side of them. Clint was standing facing the front, with Comfort between him and the door.

"Give him his gun," Comfort said.

One man stepped out of line and handed Clint his gun.

"Holster it," Comfort said.

Clint did.

"It has one bullet in it," Comfort said, with a grin. "If you can't do it with one bullet, you don't deserve your reputation."

"I could have told you that."

"What?" Comfort said.

"That I don't deserve my reputation."

Comfort frowned, not sure what Clint was trying to say.

"Listen," Clint said, "what happens if I kill you?"

Comfort shrugged.

"That's up to them, I guess," he said, indicating his men.

"Well, if I was them and you were dead, I'd recognize the fact that I wasn't going to get paid. I sure wouldn't kill someone for free."

Comfort laughed.

"You making a plea to them?" Comfort said. "You won't have to worry about that."

Clint looked at the men on his right and left, hoping that at least some of them were thinking over what he said. If he killed Comfort, he'd be easy prey for them to gun down, unless they realized that they *would* be killing him for free.

"Let's do this," Clint said. "I have a lady waiting for me."

"For you?" Comfort said. "When I'm finished here I'm going to go right up there and give her the good news."

"Come on, Comfort," Clint said, "I'm tired of talking."

Clint kept his eyes on Comfort's eyes. Peripherally, he was able to see the man's hands, and his shoulders. He had no idea how good the man was, so he needed whatever tip off he could get from the man's body, and his eyes.

For a split second Clint saw Comfort's eyes crinkle, and his shoulders hunch. Clint went for his gun then, drew it smoothly and fired one shot—the only one he had—at Comfort, and then he moved!

He did not watch to see if his shot struck Comfort. The other eight men were doing that. While they watched Comfort fall to the ground, his gun still in his holster, Clint drove his elbow into the nearest man's belly, and relieved him of his gun.

There was a shot then, and Clint didn't know where it came from. All he knew was that he wasn't hit.

A man across from him fell to the ground, apparently the victim of the shot. Clint fired at the second closest man to him, and the man went down.

Suddenly, the air in the stable was alive with lead. Clint was dimly aware that some shots were coming from above as he scrambled for cover inside a stall.

He was sitting in horse manure in the stall as the silence came. He peered out and saw that Comfort and three of his men were down. That left five men to go. He knew he had help from above them, in the hayloft, but he did not know how many people were there.

"You men listen up!" he shouted. "I told you I didn't come alone. You're outnumbered, and your boss is dead. Throw out your guns and come out with your hands raised."

He waited a few seconds, and when there was no reply he shouted, "Play it smart. Payday is over."

He waited longer this time, shifting his butt out of the horse manure, wrinkling his nose. For a split second he thought about Duke, standing out where he had left him. He wondered if the big gelding was wondering what was going on.

"All right," someone shouted, "I'm coming out."

One man stood and stepped out into view, tossing his gun ahead of him.

"Put your hands on your head," Clint instructed him, and the man obeyed.

"I'm coming out, too," someone else called, and one by one they all came out, tossed their guns to the ground and laced their fingers on their heads.

Clint stood up and stepped out, looked up above him and said, "Now who the hell is that?"

EPILOGUE

The next morning Clint, Katy and Sheriff Daniels had breakfast in the Firecreek Hotel dining room. Clint had spent the night alone. He did not know if the same could be said for Katy and Daniels.

It had been necessary for them to return to town last night in the dark. Daniels had decided not to arrest any of the men who had been in the stable and come out alive. He, Clint and Katy simply left the ranch, leaving Ben Comfort's body behind.

"What's going to happen now?" Clint asked Daniels.

"I guess that'll depend on Sam Comfort. He may still want Katy—and you—and he may now want me."

"I don't think so," Clint said.

"Why not?"

Clint took the telegram he'd received from Rick Hartman out of his pocket and handed it to Sheriff Daniels.

"He's dead."

"What?" Katy said.

"Apparently," Clint explained while Daniels read the telegram, "he took off after the posse, and out-

185

side of Denver, while he was camped, somebody robbed him and killed him. He was found a couple of days later.''

''Jesus,'' Daniels said, ''the Comforts are all gone.''

''This town has been under their thumb, hasn't it?'' Clint asked.

''Under Sam's thumb, yeah,'' Daniels said, returning the telegram. ''So have I, to tell the truth.''

''Well, now you and the town can get on with your lives.''

''I don't think so,'' Daniels said. ''Not here, anyway.''

''What do you mean?'' Clint asked.

''I mean I'm resigning.''

''When did you decide that?'' Katy asked.

''Just now,'' Daniels said. ''I might have stayed if old Sam was alive, just to prove something, but now I've got nothing to prove. I don't deserve to wear the badge, anyway.''

Clint couldn't argue that. Daniels had made a host of bad decisions, but he kept his opinion to himself.

At that point a man walked into the dining room and looked around until he found their table.

''Mr. Adams?'' he said to Clint.

''That's right.''

''Telegram, sir,'' the man said.

''Thanks,'' Clint said, taking it.

''Something important?'' Katy asked.

Clint read it, then handed it to Katy, smiling.

''Allan Pinkerton came through,'' he said. ''He's got a friend of his who is a federal judge to agree to intercede on our behalf, if we need it.''

''Which you don't,'' Daniels said. ''There are no charges. That's my last official act.''

"No," Clint said, standing up, "your last official act can be paying for breakfast."

Daniels smiled and said, "I'll do that."

"Katy," Clint said, "when you see Anne—oh, and Sandy—"

"I'll tell Anne you asked for her, Clint," Katy said.

He leaned over and kissed her on the cheek. He knew that she wasn't leaving yet, and guessed that she and Daniels were going to spend some time getting to know one another. Who knew what would happen from there?

Clint himself was heading back to Denver. He had to let Ellie know how things turned out, and he wanted to thank Pinkerton in person.

He wondered what the old curmudgeon was going to want in return.

Watch for

DEAD MAN'S JURY

ninety-sixth in the exciting
GUNSMITH series

coming in December!